To Ashley'

Aidan of Oren

The Elf Princess

Aidan of Oren
The Elf Princess

By Alan St. Jean
Illustrated by Judith Friedman

Published By Oren Village, LLC
Worthington, OH

Published by Oren Village, LLC, Worthington, Ohio. For information or permission to reproduce, please contact author@alanstjean.com or write to Alan St. Jean, PO Box 1111, Worthington, Ohio 43085. Map of Lionsgate by Judith Friedman. Text set in Berthold Garamond. Cover design by Judith Friedman. Illustrations were rendered in pen and ink with watercolor for the cover.

PUBLISHER'S CATALOGING-IN-PUBLICATION DATA
St. Jean, Alan.
Aidan of Oren : the elf princess / written by Alan St. Jean ; illustrated by Judith Friedman, Worthington, Ohio : Oren Village LLC, 2006.
p. ; cm.
ISBN-13: 978-0-9777272-0-9
ISBN-10: 0-9777272-0-3
Second installment of the Aidan of Oren trilogy.
Summary: Aidan and his friends travel to a beautiful land in search of an ancient secret. Along the way, they discover a magnificent elf princess, a curse upon the land, and an old, curious mouse that holds the key to it all.
1. Elves–Juvenile fiction. 2. Responsibility–Juvenile fiction. 3. Interpersonal relations–Juvenile fiction. 4. Heroes–Juvenile fiction. 5. Adventure stories. 6. Fantasy fiction. 7. [Fantasy.] I. Friedman, Judith, 1945–   II. Title. III. Elf princess.
PZ7.S34 A4332 2006
813.6–dc22   CIP

Table of Contents

Aidan of Oren

Prologue

It is the early morning hour. A small, nameless elf sits at an old wooden desk by candlelight. He's been writing all night, inspired by the strange events of late, heightened by word that the child of Oren soon would arrive. Small, yellowish scrolls lay scattered around him on the floor, each one representing a futile attempt to capture his thoughts. He ruffles his hair in frustration and pushes yet another scroll off of his little desk on to the floor. Why can't he get it right? It had never been this difficult before. His instincts urge him to try again. After all, he is a scribe . . . a scribe with a very special gift. Although he didn't always understand the words borne of his pen, he held true to the inspiration that moved deeply within him. Tonight, however, words eluded him. Inspiration seemed to come in short, abrupt bursts, only to be followed by echoes of emptiness. He was missing something, but what was it? The candle flickered, prompting the little elf scribe to stop writing. He put down his pen and stared thoughtfully into the soft flame. "Aidan . . . Aidan of Oren," he mused. His eyes widened and his mouth hinted of a tiny smile as new inspiration welled within him. As the flame flickered and danced, his smile grew broader. Quickly, the nameless elf picked up a fresh scroll. So furiously did his pen dance from side to side that his writing was barely legible even to himself. But he dare not slow down; there was no time for that. The fate of his village, and his people, was hanging in the balance.

CHAPTER 1

Only the Wind

The dawn of a new day broke against the horizon. Three children lay sleeping peacefully in an old stone house built on the crest of a hill overlooking a most beautiful valley . . . the Valley of the Elves.

Aidan, a boy of reddish hair and thirteen years, was the eldest of the three. His two best friends in the world were Lilly and McKenzie. Lilly, twelve years old and mature beyond her years, provided friendship as well as a stabilizing influence for Aidan. Her dark skin, black hair and penetrating, green eyes were testament to the fact that she was from a distant land. She was almost as tall as Aidan, and was every much his advisor as she was his friend. McKenzie, the beautiful and feisty fair-haired girl of seven years, was as charming as she was brave. The two girls, who had lived in the orphanage back in their humble village of Oren, had joined Aidan on a journey . . . a journey of magnificent importance and incredible danger. Joining them was Charles, Aidan's pet falcon who was often teased about being more chicken than falcon, and Damon, the white baby dragon they had found and befriended along the way.

Destiny had brought the five of them now to this magical and mysterious valley. It is here where Aidan must learn

3

about the ancient ways, and it is here where Aidan must find the guardians.

The morning skies were clear, the air was crisp and a gentle breeze whistled ever so slightly through two large oak trees guarding the eastern and western borders of the old, stone house where the children slept. The breeze found its way through the lone window of the cottage and swept across Aidan's face, causing him to stir.

"I will find you ..." he said softly, his eyes still closed. As he rolled over in bed, his face came to rest directly in front of Damon's. Damon was the baby dragon they had found a few days earlier, and was Aidan's newest friend. Although Aidan didn't wake up, Damon did. The little dragon had fallen to sleep hunched down with his head resting on Aidan's bed ... and now, he could feel Aidan's soft breath against his rounded snout. The little dragon dare not move for fear of waking the young boy. He simply lay motionless, studying Aidan's face.

Although he was not quite awake, Aidan was not quite asleep, either. A smile crossed his face, which amused the observing Damon.

"Hello, Grandmama," said Aidan. Damon's eyes opened wide with surprise, yet he remained motionless. Curious, the baby dragon moved his eyes from side to side. But no one was there. So again, Damon fixed his stare on the young boy.

Only the Wind

"Everything turned out alright, Grandmama, just like you said it would," said Aidan softly. "We followed the path, and then there were the trolls ..." His sentences were starting to break up. "You should have seen the fish ... yellow ... McKenzie was holding it in her hands. Oh, and the ... snake ... Kartha ..." His eyes were still closed, but Aidan stretched back his head as if he was looking toward something. "What a surprise ... river ... dried up ..." Aidan started laughing.

Damon continued to watch compassionately as Aidan spoke, and seemed to understand that something very special was happening. In broken sentences, Aidan recounted the amazing events of the past few days, detailing the incredible journey that he and his friends had just begun. A burst of wind blew his hair back for a moment, and then the breeze was gone. A

Aidan of Oren

Only the Wind

great peace rested on Aidan's face. "I love you, Grandmama," he said as he rolled over. "I miss you, too . . ."

Aidan of Oren

A shadow filled the room as a stranger approached the entrance of the little stone house, blocking the morning sun. "Hello? What was that I was hearing?"

Aidan sat up in bed. To his great surprise, a most beautiful girl was standing in the doorway. Her long hair sparkled golden in the morning sun, and her fair countenance was graced with pure innocence. She was fairly tall, about the same height as Aidan, who sat dumfounded in his bed not knowing what to say. Her eyes were a golden brown, soft and inviting. Lilly and McKenzie also stirred, slowly waking up.

"Hello again," said the beautiful stranger. "I thought I heard talking. Is there someone else here with you, children?"

"Only the wind," said Damon as he shuffled across the floor, past the stranger and out the door. "Only the wind."

CHAPTER 2

Olivia

idan stepped out of bed and stood awkwardly before the beautiful visitor at the door. "Hello . . ." he stammered. "Who are you?"

"My name is Olivia," she said as she looked around the room. "You must be Aidan of Oren."

"Yes," said Aidan with a hint of pride. "We've traveled a long way. It's been quite an adventure, really." He stopped for a moment as he realized that Olivia did not look like the elves they had met the night before. Rather, she looked just like them, only a little older. "Um, we just arrived last night. Where are you from?"

"Aren't you going to introduce us?" interrupted Lilly. "It's nice that she knows who you are, but I think introductions all around are in order."

"Oh, sorry," said Aidan, a little embarrassed. He walked over and stood behind the girls. "The impatient one here is Lilly," he said. "The little one with the golden hair . . . just like yours, is McKenzie."

"Her hair is not like mine!" McKenzie snapped as she turned away and folded her little arms across her chest. "I don't like her!"

"I don't think she should be here," said Lilly, also looking away.

Aidan became even more uncomfortable and started laughing nervously. "I'm not exactly sure what's happening right now. My two friends seem to have stumbled out on the wrong side of the bed this morning." Lilly shot him a warning look. "But, they're really very nice once you get to know them."

Olivia laughed softly. "Yes, I'm sure they are."

"You never said how you arrived here in the valley," said Aidan.

"Yes, and how did you know Aidan's name?" asked McKenzie suspiciously, still turned away with her arms folded in front her.

"I'm a traveler from the northern provinces. I've come a very long way . . ."

McKenzie snorted. "Hmph! Your dress is pretty clean for traveling as far as you say you have . . ."

"Hey!" interrupted Aidan. "That was a rude thing to say. How would you know, anyway? You're turned around."

"I saw enough."

"McKenzie . . ."

"It's certainly alright," said Olivia. "I would probably be upset, too, if my best friend was making a new friend. Anyway, I was headed south when I passed by a tree stump with a little red door. It was open, and I was immensely curious, so I entered. It's almost as if I chose a path of destiny."

Olivia

MY NAME IS OLIVIA

Aidan did not know what to say, but Lilly did. She turned to face Olivia, and was stopped momentarily by her sheer beauty. But she shook it off. "Someone told me that destiny chooses it's own, Olivia. I don't think it happens the other way around."

Olivia stepped back. "I didn't mean to say . . ."

"It's alright," said Aidan, trying to make peace. "The fact is that you're here, and I believe we have a pretty big day ahead of us."

"Well, don't mind me," said Olivia. "I'm just here to watch. I'll be quiet and let you do whatever it is that you're supposed to do here."

"See?" said Aidan to Lilly and McKenzie. "She's harmless. Rather than fighting, why don't we prepare ourselves to meet the elves . . . I'm sure they'll be here soon to take us to their village."

This made the girls perk up, and even awoke Charles, Aidan's pet falcon, who had been sleeping on the rail at the foot of Aidan's bed.

"What's going on, here?" he said, still a little groggy. "And who is this . . . this . . . *beautiful* creature before me?"

Olivia blushed, but Lilly and McKenzie just rolled their eyes.

"Oh, what a clever little bird," said Olivia as she walked over to pet Charles on the head.

The proud falcon puffed out his chest and warmly accepted the attention from the stranger. "You know, I'm not just a mere bird . . ."

"Oh, what a clever little bird!"

"There's no time to go into that now," said Aidan. "I think I hear footsteps!" The children hushed and listened. Tiny footsteps could be heard, just like Aidan said, and they were getting closer.

"They're coming!" exclaimed McKenzie as she rushed around the room to get her things. "I hope I get to see Frederick again!"

"Oh, my . . ." said Lilly as she, too, rushed to straighten up.

Aidan of Oren

Olivia quietly slipped outside. Aidan finished tying off the bands of his new shirt the elves had given him and moved towards the door. He paused when he heard a familiar voice. It was Sebastian Fry, the leader of the elves. As Aidan peeked around the corner, he saw Sebastian and Sprite, a small female elf, petting and talking softly to Damon. Aidan motioned for Lilly and McKenzie to stand beside him, and the three children watched as the two elves seemed to be having a pleasant discussion with the white baby dragon.

"Hello, Sebastian Fry!" said McKenzie as she pushed her way through the door. "Did you bring Frederick with you?" Frederick was the child elf she had met and befriended the day earlier.

The leader of the elves turned to greet her.

'Good morning to you
Little one fair
We hope you slept well
In the cool night air
It's time for the journey
And time for the fates
Let's head to the village
Where Frederick awaits'

Aidan, with Charles on his shoulder, and Lilly followed McKenzie out of the little house to greet the elves. Just as they stepped outside, Aidan grabbed Lilly's arm. He pointed toward the twin-mountains that reached for the sky. "Look, Lilly, do you see that?"

"I do," she said. "Isn't it beautiful?"

"Of course it's beautiful!" Aidan said, a little flustered. "But, we know that only one mountain really stands . . . right?"

"Yes," Lilly smiled. "But we're not from here, are we?"

"No, I don't suppose so," Aidan stammered. "But we didn't go far . . . last night at the tree stump, we just passed through a little red door. How did that mountain get there?"

McKenzie walked back to where Aidan and Lilly were standing and took Aidan's hand. "C'mon, Aidan, let's go! Didn't you hear what Sebastian Fry said the day before? He said that this was a place of *when*, not *where*! We've been taken to a time before the mountain was destroyed!" The little seven year old with the beautiful, blond hair pulled Aidan and Lilly up to meet Sebastian Fry.

"Why is it so easy for her?" an exasperated Aidan whispered under his breath in Lilly's direction. He then righted himself as he came to stand before the leader of the elves. "Good morning, Sebastian." He looked back toward the stone building where they had slept. "Did you meet Olivia? She was just talking to us and . . ." Sebastian Fry looked all around and then at Sprite, who slowly shook her head. He turned to Aidan with a blank expression. "Olivia, the tall woman with the long, fair hair. She was just here." But there was no one else. Aidan and the children searched the entire area, calling for the stranger, but Olivia was nowhere to be found.

CHAPTER 3

The Shadow

ebastian Fry took Aidan's hand and proceeded to lead him toward the top of the crest. Lilly and McKenzie followed, but kept looking back toward the house, wondering about the strange Olivia who had seemed to simply disappear. Sprite, who was not much taller than Damon, took the little dragon's hand and led him along just behind the two girls. As they reached the crest, the children froze in amazement. The valley before them bore more beauty than they had ever seen. Thousands of little stone houses, smaller than the one they had slept in, dotted the undulating landscape. The morning sun glistened off of the straw rooftops, still moist from the previous night's dew.

"Paradise!" Aidan exclaimed.

Lilly held both hands over her mouth, gasping at the wonder before them. "I can't believe it . . ."

"Paradise, indeed . . ." mused Charles. "What a delightful change to that dreadful forest. Maybe now we'll be able to get a little peace and quiet."

McKenzie did not say a word. Rather, she studied Sebastian Fry's little face. One would think that the elf leader would be most proud to show off his home. Rather, he bore a look of utmost concern. He turned toward the children.

'Paradise lives while there is light
'Tis not the same when comes the night'

"Don't start talking nonsense!" cried Charles. "We haven't even been here a day and . . . mmmph mmph!"

Aidan reached up and stopped the falcon from talking further. "I'm sorry about Charles," he said. "He

scares easily. But, just what did you mean regarding the night?"

Sebastian Fry motioned for the children to follow him down a winding path leading into the valley. As they were walking, he told them a story.

'It used to be when I was small
Delightful days and nights, them all
And then, we know not why, but when
A Shadow came into the glen
Children, many, disappeared
Women wept, strong men feared
Striking only in the dark
It fears the day and candle spark
And so in every home at night
We all must hide by candlelight'

"Incredible . . ." said Aidan soberly. "How long have you been living like this?"

The time to sum up all the fears
Is two plus two, plus three more years'

"What?" said Aidan, scratching his head.

"Seven years," said McKenzie. "You have to do the math."

Charles, determined not to hear any more of it, dug his head deeper into Aidan's collar.

"Everything seems so beautiful," said Lilly. "I can't believe that something so dreadful could exist here." Sebastian Fry nodded slowly, confirming the fact that this was indeed a most serious matter. The little elf continued on in silence. A cloud of concern hovered over them all and choked away their short-lived excitement.

Even so, Aidan was determined to learn more about the mystery.

"Sebastian, why do they call it a shadow if it only comes at night?"

McKenzie tugged on his sleeve and put her little finger over her lips, silencing him. "This is something they don't like to talk about," she whispered. "But, to answer your question, what better time for a shadow to attack than at night?"

"But," Aidan whispered. "A shadow couldn't be seen at night."

"Exactly," McKenzie said as she tried to wink.

"I'm not listening," whimpered Charles from under Aidan's collar. "I will not hear this ... I'm not listening!"

CHAPTER 4

Noam

As the children drew closer to the city, it became obvious that something very special was in the air. The little elves that lived in the village were scurrying all about. Some of the elves were decorating their houses with long strands of braided flowers. Others could be seen practicing tumbling and juggling. Entering the center of the village, the group led by Sebastian Fry turned to the left, which pointed them down a much wider street. There was a post on the corner of this street with a board nailed to it. A single word, 'Haven', was carved into the board.

"The Haven," whispered McKenzie. "I've heard of this place . . ."

Small buildings lined each side of the street in the Haven, each unique in design and purpose. In one of the buildings, an elf could be seen forming clay to create plates and bowls. In another, a muscular elf was forging iron with a hammer. Yet another revealed a number of elves inside, weaving baskets.

Aidan watched in awe as elves, coming from all directions, would approach the small shops. One elf went to the pottery maker and was handed two plates. Another stepped into the basket shop and came out with beautiful baskets. There was no exchange of gold or silver. Rather, each need was met with a smile and a handshake.

THE HAVEN

Sebastian Fry walked up to one of the little buildings and caught the attention of those inside. He pointed back down the street and started talking to them.

'It's time to get the tables
Please put them in a line
Call all of the musicians
And don't forget the wine
The celebration's close at hand

Aidan of Oren

All we need is one
The princess will be coming
Before the setting sun'

"The Princess!" squealed McKenzie. "She's coming!"

"Who's coming?" asked Aidan and Lilly together.

"The Elf Princess! She rules the elves in solitude from a place called Labyrinth. It is very rare for her to show herself! In fact, no one alive has ever seen her! Sebastian says that she's coming today!"

"I thought Sebastian Fry ruled the elves," said Aidan, scratching his head.

"No, silly!" smirked McKenzie. "He's the *leader* of the Elves. A leader and a ruler are two different things."

Aidan slowly nodded, but his face clearly showed that he didn't understand. McKenzie softened a little and explained further.

"As leader of the elves, Sebastian Fry makes the laws and governs the people. The Elf Princess, however, brings healing and joy." McKenzie squinted her eyes in an attempt to look mysterious. "Some even say she brings the sunlight."

"I like that story," said Lilly. "But why is she coming now?"

Sebastian Fry interrupted them, motioning for them to continue following him down the street. As they were walking, Aidan looked back and noticed a group of elves bringing tables and placing them end-to-end. They were formed in a straight line down the middle of the street.

"It looks like they're preparing for a great feast," said Lilly. "I'm sure it's because the Elf Princess is coming."

"Food?" Charles finally popped his head up out of Aidan's collar. "It's about time they fed us . . . I'm starving!"

Aidan chuckled and looked down to check on Damon. The little dragon was perfectly content walking beside Sprite, who still held his little hand in hers.

"It looks like Damon made a new friend," he whispered to Lilly. "She's just his size . . ."

"Excuse me," interrupted Charles. "I don't trust these little people. What if they're not really as nice as they seem? What if they're hiding something? Hmm?"

"Yeah . . ." echoed McKenzie. "And, what if *we* are the main course for tonight's feast!"

"Stop it!" shrieked Charles. The children laughed. Aidan reached up and gently petted his cowardly friend and whispered reassuring words to him. Suddenly, he noticed that the road had come to a dead end.

"What . . .?" he started to ask. The road ended in front of a fairly large stone building, surrounded by steps. There was only one entrance . . . a large, wooden door that looked very old. Above the door, strange writing was chiseled in stone. Sebastian Fry turned towards Aidan, who was dumbfounded by what he saw. The little elf pointed toward the writing.

"This building looks familiar," said Aidan mysteriously. "But I don't recognize the writing above the door."

"Those are letters from the elf alphabet," said McKenzie.

"Well," said Aidan anxiously. "What does it say?"

"I can't read it," said McKenzie as she started giggling. "After all, I am only seven, you know."

"Yes, but you seem to know a lot about . . ."

The conversation was interrupted by the sound of very loud, squeaky hinges.

"The door!" shouted Lilly. "It's opening!" Indeed, the door to the stone building was opening, revealing an interior as black as night. The children watched in silence as a shadowy figure slowly emerged from inside.

"It's a rat!" exclaimed Aidan.

"No," said McKenzie. "It is a mouse. It's just big . . . for a mouse."

"I would have to agree with McKenzie," chimed Lilly. "Rat is such a dirty word, it might be offensive . . ."

The strange mouse slowly made its way down the steps toward the children. A most magnificent creature, it stood upright and was almost as tall as McKenzie. It had curious spectacles that framed its small, beady eyes and a perceptive, twitchy little nose. Its front arms were short, causing him to hold his hands closely in front of its chest. Its toes and fingers were long and gnarly, often crossing nervously.

The mouse first approached Lilly. She stood motionless as the creature reached up and touched her beautiful black hair. Then, the mouse noticed her basket and started to lift the lid.

Noam

"Hey!" said Lilly, pulling the basket away. "That's not yours!"

The mouse was not startled. Rather, it motioned for the basket. "Pleeeease?" it said in a strange, crackling voice. Lilly did not respond, so the mouse grinned, revealing it's two large, yellowy front teeth to show it was friendly.

"Eew!" said Lilly as she opened the lid of her basket and held it out toward the mouse. "Here, take what you want."

As the mouse rooted through the basket, Aidan noticed that Sebastian Fry was observing everything very proudly. This made him feel more at ease.

The mouse, gnawing on a small loaf of bread it had found in the basket, turned toward McKenzie. She smiled at the creature, took its little hands in hers, and bowed halfway.

"It's nice to meet you, mister mouse," she said. The mouse, still holding on to the bread, instinctively pulled back. This made McKenzie laugh. "Don't worry, I don't want your food." The brave seven year old then reached out and patted the mouse on his long, twitching nose. "What is your name?"

The twitching stopped. The strange mouse cocked its head slightly to the side as he replied. "Noam. Yes, my name is Noam."

Noam bent to the side and peered around McKenzie. Damon, who was sitting behind her, made eye contact with the strange mouse. Noam stepped forward and bent over, cautiously placing a trembling hand on top of Damon's head. "Ohhhh . . . so you *do* exist . . . yes, you most certainly do . . .".

Aidan, trying not to laugh, nudged Lilly and whispered, "I think he's scared of Damon!"

Noam straightened up and turned toward Aidan. "Aren't you?" The mouse took a big bite out of the loaf of bread and pointed toward the stone building. "The Hall of Judges," he said with his mouth full of food.

"What do you mean?" asked Aidan.

"The writing," said the mouse between bites, motioning to the building behind him. "Above the door. The Hall of Judges".

"That's the name of the building back in Oren!" exclaimed Aidan. "Now that I think about it, it even *looks* like the one in Oren, only this one's much smaller and not all boarded up."

"My home . . . yes, my home," said Noam proudly, still chewing. Then he swallowed very loud and looked Aidan right in the eye. "Welcome."

"YES, MY NAME IS NOAM"

CHAPTER 5

The Dragon Chest

Startled, Aidan took a step back as the otherwise timid Noam seemed to look right through him. Before he could answer, he was interrupted by a familiar voice.

"Hello . . . I was looking all over for you!"

"Olivia!" exclaimed Aidan as the familiar stranger made her way down the wide street toward the children. Lilly and McKenzie turned to greet Olivia as well, although not with the same enthusiasm as Aidan had shown. Sebastian Fry, who stood next to Noam, looked puzzled.

"Sebastian Fry, I'd like you to meet Olivia. She came through the little red door, just like we did." The leader of the elves continued to stare blankly at Olivia.

"Fry, is it possible . . . yes, is it possible that you left the door open last night?" asked Noam, who's nose started twitching again. Sebastian shrugged his shoulders.

'I thought that I had shut the door
As we walked through the tree

28

The Dragon Chest

"IS IT POSSIBLE THAT YOU LEFT THE DOOR OPEN LAST NIGHT?"

But, maybe, when I came for more
I left it wide for all to see'

"Could anything else have come through the door?" asked McKenzie.

"You mean, *anyone* else," corrected Aidan. McKenzie just looked away.

Aidan turned to Noam and repeated McKenzie's question. Noam did not answer. Rather, he turned his attention to Sebastian Fry.

"Fry, let's show our guests around the village. Groups . . . yes, let's go in groups."

The little elf nodded and turned to the children.

'Warrior and Sprite, walk to the right
Frederick will meet you where rocks take flight
Lilly and Damon, come with me

Aidan of Oren

We'll go left to the Arboree
Aidan, Charles, go with Noam
He has invited you to his home'

"That dreadful building? I'm not going in there!" squawked Charles.

"What about Olivia?" asked Aidan, ignoring the falcon. "Whom should she go with?"

"Thank you for thinking of me," said Olivia, stepping into the middle of the group. "I'd be perfectly happy joining you and the mouse person in the . . ."

"She can come with me!" interrupted McKenzie.

"But . . ." protested Olivia. It was of no use. McKenzie grabbed her hand and locked arms with Sprite, then whisked them off to the right in search of Frederick, and to the place where rocks take flight.

Lilly started laughing.

"What's so funny?" asked Aidan. "I can't believe McKenzie wants to make friends with Olivia. That's quite a switch from earlier this morning."

"Maybe she just wants to keep an eye on her," said Lilly with a wink.

"Oh, stop it," said Aidan, getting a little perturbed. "You two are just jealous because she's older, taller and prettier . . ."

Lilly folded her arms together in defiance and walked away. "Sebastian Fry! I'm ready to go!" The little leader of the elves quickly snapped to attention and escorted Lilly and Damon to the left, where they would discover the magnificent shade trees of the Arboree.

"Oh, Aidan," Charles whispered in his ear. "You really need to learn when to *shut up*." Aidan, not wanting to hear any more, grabbed the falcon's beak and followed Noam up the steps and toward the large door of the Hall of Judges.

Just as he reached the door, the curious mouse stopped and looked up toward the sun, then down at his feet. "Hmm ... what do you see, Aidan of Oren?"

"I see your feet," said Aidan jokingly. "And, they're not pretty!"

Noam did not react to the poor attempt at humor. "What else do you see?"

"Um," Aidan cleared his throat nervously as he could tell the mouse was not amused. "I see your shadow?"

"Exactly," said Noam as he turned toward the door. "Isn't it curious how easily a shadow can be seen during the day?" Aidan just scratched his head and followed close behind. As they entered the stone building, Noam cautioned them.

"Step inside and stop," he said as he closed the door behind them. "It will take a moment for your eyes to adjust to the dim lighting. I like it in here. Outside's much too bright, much too bright."

It was hard to see with the door closed, but Aidan could see enough to know that the curious mouse had moved to the center of the room, where a solitary ray of light peered through a small hole in the roof, lighting only the spot where Noam was standing. As his eyes adjusted, it became clear that they were standing in a library. Rows and rows of books on old wooden shelves were placed along the outside walls of the stone building, which was nothing more than one large room. There was a solitary table in the center of the building beside Noam. Aidan could see something on top of the table, but it appeared to be covered with a sheet. Crude iron and wooden tools lay on both sides of the mysterious object.

"Just a moment," said Noam as he peeked under the sheet. He looked back at Aidan as if to make sure he hadn't moved, and then again peeked under the sheet. "Yes . . . yes . . . almost ready . . . almost," he said mysteriously.

"What's under the sheet?" asked Aidan as his eyes began adjusting to the dim lighting.

"Well," said Noam, standing upright and turning around. "It's just a little project . . . yes, just a little project I've been working on."

"How long have you been working on it?"

"Oh, let me see . . . let me see, about seven years." His little nose started twitching as he patted the covered object with one hand. "Do you want to come see it?"

Aidan moved toward the center of the room where Noam stood next to the mysterious object. Charles started to protest, but Aidan would have none of it.

"Go ahead," said Noam. "Remove the sheet."

The Dragon Chest

"Alright," said Aidan as he slowly pulled the white piece of linen off of the object. The top surface was somewhat rough and snagged the sheet. Aidan reached over and pulled the sheet off of what appeared to be a tree branch, then ran his hand over the top of the object. He gasped as the sheet fell to the floor. "A chest!"

"Is something wrong?" asked Noam. "Why did you stop?"

It was all Aidan could do to step away from the object. He was trembling.

"Don't you like it?" asked Noam mysteriously. "I would hate to think . . . yes, hate to think, that you, of all people, would not like it."

Aidan reached forward and put his hand on the front of the chest. He traced the carvings of the two dragons, one white, the other black, facing each other. "This is Grandmama's dragon chest!" he exclaimed.

Noam did not say a word.

"Seven years to make this . . ." said Aidan as he continued to run his hands over the chest. "Seven years. Where have I heard that before?" He turned toward Noam. "Why are you building this chest?"

The strange mouse clapped his little hands together tightly. "Because there is a need!"

"But . . . why would it take so long just to build a chest?"

"There is much . . . yes, much, that you do not understand," said Noam. "This is not just a chest. No . . . it is a vessel."

"For what?"

"A vessel for good," said the curious mouse, flashing his yellowish grin. Then Noam's small, beady eyes locked with Aidan's. "And evil."

Chapter 6

Elijah

Charles could remain silent no longer. "Please!" he whined. "Stop speaking so dramatically! After all, we're just talking about a big wooden box!" The falcon boldly puffed up his chest. "Now, tell me, my twitchy friend, exactly what will you put in this *oh-so-mysterious* box?"

Noam turned away. "All in good time. Yes, all in good time."

"Oh, there he goes again, Aidan!" cried Charles. "All of this suspense and wild talk about shadows and good and evil and such. Why, there's nothing at all scary about this place!"

Aidan, ignoring the ranting falcon, was drawn back to the chest. He found himself admiring its craftsmanship, and he wondered at the carvings of the eyes between the branches that lined the lid.

His thoughts were interrupted. "Your training begins . . . yes, begins today," said the curious mouse. "The chest before you was created from two basic materials. Two materials that are actually one."

"Oh, *please* . . ." sighed Charles.

"Quiet!" scolded Aidan. "This is important." He turned to Noam. "What two materials are you talking about?" Aidan walked around the chest, examining it carefully. He slowly lifted the lid and looked inside. "I see only wood."

"Ha!" shouted Noam, startling Aidan. "Wood, yes . . . but two very different types. It is most important *why*."

"What do you mean?" asked Aidan as Charles sighed heavily. "Oak? Birch? I wouldn't even know where to start guessing . . ."

"You look with your eyes rather than with your heart. Look again."

Aidan studied the trunk. The branches forming the lid were a different shade than the wood forming the base. Then he saw it . . . a small bud starting to flower on one of the lids branches.

"They're alive!" he shouted. "The branches forming the lid are alive!" He reached his hand again over the top of the chest. "The wood forming the base is hewn and formed into planks, but the branches forming the lid are flexible. How is this possible?"

"I told you . . . it took me seven years . . . yes, seven years."

"Oh, poppycock!" shouted Charles. "Maybe you just placed new branches on the top of the lid today to give the appearance that they were alive!"

"Yes," said Noam mysteriously. "And, maybe I laid them in place six and a half years ago . . ."

Elijah

Charles tossed his head in the other direction, ignoring the comment.

"Do the live branches have anything to do with the carvings of the eyes?" asked Aidan.

"Ha! Of course, my young apprentice. If the chest were not alive . . . it wouldn't need to see. No, it wouldn't need to see at all."

"No, no, no!" shouted Charles. "You are *not* telling us that this . . . this abomination can *see* us!"

"Why, yes . . . yes, that's exactly what I'm saying. In fact, it's been watching you since you came into the room."

"Aidan!" shrieked Charles.

Noam flashed a big grin in Aidan's direction as if he were very pleased with himself.

"What does this have to do with my training?" asked Aidan. "I'm not sure of the lesson here."

"You'll be sure . . . yes, very sure," said Noam as he picked the sheet up off of the floor. "Wait here." The curious mouse moved over to the corner of the room behind a bookshelf.

"Where is he going?" asked Charles impatiently. "I can hear him shuffling around." Charles glanced over to the chest, which by now was starting to give him the chills. "I want to leave now."

"Shh!" whispered Aidan. "I think this is important."

Before Charles could say another word, they both noticed a shuffling sound coming toward them.

"It's the mouse!" cried Charles. "Look, he's put the sheet over his head! What kind of game is this?"

Sure enough, Noam had apparently put the sheet over his head and was heading toward Aidan and Charles.

"Who am I?" they heard.

Aidan stepped back.

"Oh, don't be such a sissy!" cried Charles. "It appears that our rodent friend is simply attempting a little ghostly humor."

"Something's not right," said Aidan.

"Who am I?" they heard again, this time the voice echoed all around the room.

Aidan gulped. "Why, you're Noam, of course."

"Are you sure?" came the voice as the figure moved even closer.

"Of course I'm sure," said Aidan, gathering his courage. "And, I think I understand the lesson here. Even though I can't see your face, I know it's you and I shouldn't be afraid simply because there's a veil of mystery separating us."

The figure stopped in front of him as silence filled the room.

"Oh, just pull the sheet off and let's be on with it!" said Charles. "This game is getting a little boring!"

Aidan reached over and pulled off the sheet. To his horror, the creature underneath was not Noam! It was a large, most frightening beast covered with clumps of matted hair. Its disturbing head bore more teeth than face. Large, white eyes contained very small pupils, giving the beast an almost crazed appearance, and it was breathing hard. Aidan heard a soft gasp coming from

Elijah

his left shoulder, followed by a dull thud. He realized that Charles had fainted and fallen to the floor, but he could do nothing about that now.

The creature moved closer to Aidan. He gasped as he noticed its long, dangling arms, ending with large, meaty hands which drug beside it on the ground. Its mouth was open and slightly drooling. Aidan, trying desperately to think, dared not move. The creature was now face to face with him. A long, beet red tongue emerged from the creature's huge mouth and rubbed up against his face.

"He likes you," said Noam as he stepped around the bookcase.

Aidan's expression turned from fear to disgust. "Hopefully not to eat," he said, trying his best to maintain a sense of humor. "You may have scared Charles to death, you know."

"The bird will be fine . . . yes, fine," said Noam as he walked up behind the creature and fastened an iron collar to its neck. The collar was attached to a long, heavy chain.

"Noam, what kind of creature is this? Why do you keep him in chains?"

"The creature has a name, Aidan. Yes, his name is *Elijah*. He is from the line of the Cuchulainn, and as far as I know he is the very last of his kind."

"Cuchulainn?"

"There is a legend passed on through the centuries . . . a legend of one called Cuchulainn. He was a devastating creature of war. Fearless, as you might imagine.

Elijah

HIS NAME IS ELIJAH

Yes, fearless. He was also very handsome, very hand-some indeed, that is, when he wasn't fighting." Aidan hung on every word as Noam continued the story. "However, when provoked, Cuchulainn changed in a most horrifying way. His face became misshapen, and his body assumed the stature of a beast. He was un-stoppable, destroying all in his path. That was long ago. For some reason, the offspring of Cuchulainn were not as fair to look upon. They inherited only the character-istics of Cuchulainn as a war creature, hideous and dif-ferent from other species. It is for this reason that they have been tragically, so tragically, misunderstood. Yes, they have even been hunted and killed." Noam reached up with his little arms and patted the creature on the back. "Come, Elijah . . . yes, you are a good boy. Let's put you back to bed."

The creature obliged as Noam proceeded to lead him toward the bookcase. Suddenly, the beast stopped and looked back at the unconscious falcon lying on the floor. It licked its lips slowly.

"Hey!" shouted Aidan. "That's my friend!"

The creature quickly turned around and followed Noam out of sight. Aidan bent down and gently picked up Charles and laid him on the table, next to the chest. The falcon was breathing softly, and did not appear to have been hurt by the fall.

"What did you think of Elijah?" asked Noam as he re-entered the room.

"Why do you bind the creature with a heavy chain?" asked Aidan as he turned around. "Is he your friend?"

"His name is Elijah," said the mouse, a little perturbed. "And yes . . . yes, he is my friend."

"Then, again, why do you bind him in chains?"

"Oh, that must have been a bit disconcerting to you. The fact is that Elijah is very strong . . . and wild. Yes, he will always be wild. He guards the library . . . a very important job. Hmmm . . . very important."

"If he's wild, then why did you allow him in the room with us?"

"Oh, he would not hurt you, Aidan of Oren. He senses that you are great . . . yes, he has very good senses . . ."

Elijah

"What about Charles, then? I don't like the way he was looking at him."

Charles stirred, slowly lifting his head to make sense out of what was being said.

"Oh, the falcon . . . yes, Elijah would love to eat him," replied Noam candidly.

"Ah!" whimpered Charles, his eyes rolling back in his head and again going unconscious.

"No!" shouted Aidan. "He is not allowed eat my friend!"

"Alright . . ." said Noam. "But I'll have to write that down. Hmmm, let's see, where's my quill pen? Ha! I can never find it when I need it." He stopped abruptly and looked at Aidan. His nose started twitching. "You learned a valuable lesson today."

Aidan shook his head. "I don't know about that. All I know is, if I had looked harder, I would have seen your friend's knuckles dragging beside his feet."

"His name is Elijah . . ."

"I know, I know. And, if I had listened closer, I would have realized that the voice was coming from somewhere else in the room."

Noam's nose started twitching faster. "What else did you learn?"

"I'm not sure what you mean . . ."

"You hesitated."

Aidan began to shuffle his feet nervously. "Yes, when I heard the voice echoing around the room, I thought something wasn't right."

"Exactly!" said Noam. "When you sensed something was wrong, why didn't you look closer? Yes, you would have seen the knuckles dragging. You may have even heard his breath under the sheet. Listen with your heart, my boy."

"I've heard that before . . ."

"And never forget it!" exclaimed Noam. "For it would surely be your undoing."

The room became silent. No one had ever spoken to Aidan in such a manner. Fear gripped his heart as he remembered the true reason why he was there. Aidan was the one prophesied to end the war that ravaged his homeland. He was afraid of failing his friends, and his country.

"Don't be afraid," said Noam thoughtfully. "Replace your fear with determination. Yes . . . determination and focus."

Aidan turned around and started walking toward the back of the stone building. "How can I not be afraid?" he asked. "My friends, you, and all of Lionsgate are depending on me. I don't know how to focus. I don't even know what I'm supposed to do."

"Of course you do," said Noam, following behind. "But, you need to start now. Ask questions . . . many questions, and consider those things that are not obvious. And never assume that anything is what it seems to be. Rather, prove all things."

"What do you mean, ask questions? I don't have any questions . . ."

"I think you do," replied Noam. "You've just covered them with assumptions. Ha! Look under the sheet if you dare!"

Aidan had a puzzled look on his face.

"In fact," continued the mysterious mouse, "I think you have *many* questions."

CHAPTER 7

The Elf Princess

Their conversation was interrupted by the sound of musical instruments.

"Where is that music coming from?" asked Aidan.

"See?" said Noam, again flashing his yellowish grin. "You asked a question!"

Charles started to awaken. "Where ... where in blazes am I?" he demanded.

"There's no time for that, now," said Aidan as he whisked the falcon off the table and onto his shoulder. Let's go see what's happening outside!"

Noam led the way to the door and slowly opened it, revealing the blinding light of day.

"I can hardly see," said Aidan, putting his hand up to block the unyielding sun. He walked down a few steps and looked around. "The music is getting louder. Something's definitely coming." He turned to see that Noam had started to make his way back inside the door.

"Where are you going?" asked Aidan in a panic.

"Ha!" said Noam as he turned to close the door.

"You asked another question! Keep asking them, young Aidan. Don't be afraid to ask the hard ones."

"But," cried Aidan as the door started to close. "How can I ask you questions if you're not with me?" He quickly slid his foot inside the door to keep it from closing. Noam's nose and whiskers peeked out through the opening, right in Aidan's face.

"It's not important to whom you ask the questions . . . only that you ask the questions."

"But, when? When do I ask the questions?"

The mouse's whiskers were tickling Aidan's cheek as he whispered. "Always ask questions. But when the time is within the time, then you will know it's time to ask the hard question."

"What does that mean?" Aidan removed his foot from the door.

"It means exactly what it means, young Aidan. When the time is within the time. Don't worry, you'll know!"

Thud! The door closed. Noam's voice had gone silent. Aidan turned his head and looked at Charles, who was glaring at him. The falcon cleared his throat, and then spoke slowly and in a very dry voice. "Don't you ever, *ever* take me back in there."

Aidan slowly descended down the steps and proceeded up the street of the haven. The music was getting louder. Suddenly, Aidan heard footsteps behind him. He turned just in time to catch McKenzie jumping in his arms. "She's coming! She's coming now!"

squealed the excited seven-year old. "The music that you hear is being played by the best elf musicians in the land!"

Aidan put McKenzie down and could see that she was not alone. Lilly, Damon, Sebastian Fry and little Frederick followed behind. He took McKenzie's cheeks in his hands. "You will never believe what I saw in that building . . ."

"Not now!" said McKenzie as she pulled away and continued walking up the street.

"She's right," said Lilly as she approached Aidan. "We also have seen some strange things today. There will be much to talk about tonight. But for now, I think something amazing is about to happen."

Aidan noticed that Sebastian Fry, Damon and Frederick had followed McKenzie up the street. With a wink, he grabbed Lilly's hand the two of them ran to catch up with the group. They all stopped in front of the building where baskets were made, for around the corner they could see the first few musicians of what seemed to be an oncoming parade. The music was unlike any that the children had ever heard before. Harmonies from a multitude of stringed instruments were delicately woven with the precise plucking of harps. Soft wind instruments could also be heard, sounding somewhat like flutes and oboes. It was soothing, yet contained an air of excitement. Lilly and McKenzie were talking quietly together and laughing in anticipation of the Elf Princess, who was about to appear.

The Elf Princess

Aidan's attention was broken as the door to the basket shop opened slowly. A female elf emerged, holding the hands of two elf children that seemed to be squabbling over a small basket. She led them out into the street, trying desperately to turn their attention toward the oncoming parade. Her efforts were in vain, however, for the children, each holding on to the basket, were obsessed with having the woven prize for their own. Their antics amused Aidan, as he recalled similar quarrels with Lilly and McKenzie when they were younger. He looked down the street, noting that the tables that had been lined up were now graced with all kinds of fruit and bread. The tableware, which shimmered in the afternoon sun, looked to be made of pure silver. Everything was perfect. The two elf children, still fighting over the basket, fell over each other in the street and accidentally bumped into one of the tables.

The crowd hushed. Even the two children stopped suddenly and turned their attention down the street. Aidan looked up just in time to notice a sight he would never forget. Four stout little elves came around the corner at the base of the street carrying a most magnificent chair, one woven by nature itself. Even more magnificent was the one sitting in the chair. "The Elf Princess!" he gasped. The elves that bore her chair stopped. She gracefully stood and faced the elves that swarmed around her. Her long, dark hair and wispy clothing blew gently in the wind as she stood in silence, lovingly laying her hands on the heads of those closest

50

to her. She was taller than all of the elves. Her eyes were large, dark and piercing.

As she began to slowly make her way up the street, the little elf band started playing again. Laughter filled the Haven as the elves pressed in to be close to the Princess. Without saying a word, she walked up to McKenzie and Lilly and nodded approvingly.

"I don't know what all the fuss is about . . ." started Charles.

"Not now, Charles. Not now," whispered Aidan.

The Elf Princess approached Aidan and Sebastian Fry. Aidan didn't know what to say. He felt awkward. Sebastian Fry stepped forward.

'We welcome you with open arms
You grace our home with warmth and charm
This stranger from a distant land
Wishes now to kiss your hand'

"What?" cried Aidan, completely startled as the Elf Princess slowly offered her hand. Sebastian Fry reached back and pulled Aidan forward, motioning with his head that this was something Aidan needed to do . . . and now.

Aidan reached for the Elf Princess' delicate white hand and kissed it softly. He looked up to see her gazing right through him. Although again startled, he maintained his composure and stepped backward, bowing slightly in an attempt to be polite.

The Elf Princess raised her hands and turned around, which silenced the crowd and the band.

The Elf Princess

'You honor me in word and deed
I want for not a thing
Your hearts are filled with goodness
From afar I hear you sing
And so, tonight, let's celebrate
The coming of the one
Prophesied to end the curse
And fill the Shadow with the sun'

Chapter 8

Frederick the Juggler

ill the Shadow with the sun?" asked Aidan. "Sebastian, what does she mean?"

The leader of the elves clapped his hands three times and shouted:

The time has come to sit and feast
Let every man and every beast
Take this time to share and laugh
Come near, come far, from yonder path
Jesters that play, and singers that hum
Take your place in the show to come
All others, please, move in stride
And now be seated at the table side'

Even as Sebastian Fry finished his last words, elves started moving in from all directions. They were coming to the Haven to sit at the table for the great celebration. Other elves could be seen walking toward them in groups. Aidan could hear some of the groups singing softly together. Other groups could be seen juggling strange objects; practicing for the events to come.

Most of the elves were bringing small chairs and seating themselves at the table. Since the tables were so low, Aidan, Lilly and McKenzie sat on the ground next to them. The Elf Princess had returned to her chair, which was now seated at the far end of the table where the Haven began. Once she started eating, all of the elves started helping themselves to the bounty of food before them. The children, still trying to make sense of their surroundings, started eating as well. They watched with amusement as the elves put on a musical production planned long ago for this very occasion. Court jesters, acting silly, kept the elf crowd laughing between songs.

Then, in a touching moment, little Frederick approached the Elf Princess and bowed. He pulled three peculiar bluish stones out of his pocket and attempted, with very little success, to juggle them. Aidan and the girls watched in tender amusement as Frederick tried time and time again to successfully juggle the stones, only to drop them repeatedly on the ground. The Elf Princess started clapping softly, and soon everyone seated at all of the tables clapped also, giving little Frederick a well deserved ovation.

"What an amazing day this has been," whispered Lilly to Aidan.

"I agree!" blurted in McKenzie between bites of a small loaf of bread in her hands. "It has been a day I will never forget!"

"Shhh!" scolded Lilly. "Quiet! They're trying to put on a show for the Princess!"

"Her name is Lira," whispered McKenzie. "Isn't that the most beautiful name you've ever heard?"

Aidan of Oren

Charles hopped off of Aidan's shoulder and walked over beside McKenzie who, in her excitement, was dropping crumbs everywhere. Damon sat across from Aidan, next to Sprite. Aidan noticed that the little dragon seemed to watch all of the activities with great interest.

"What are you thinking, Damon?" he asked.

Damon cocked his head to the side. "I'm learning . . ." he said, and then redirected his attention back to the elves.

Aidan laughed. Although his head was still spinning from the events of the day, his attention was drawn to Sebastian Fry, now seated silently beside him. The little leader of the elves was not eating. Rather, he looked away as if he was sad. His thoughts were obviously somewhere else.

"Sebastian," said Aidan. "What's wrong? This is supposed to be a day of celebration."

The little elf stared straight forward, not saying a word.

"Come on," coaxed Aidan. "I heard what Lira said. What's this about filling the Shadow with the sun?" He laughed, trying to make light of the situation. "I'm supposed to be here to learn something . . . you know, I'm getting tired of playing the hero . . ."

Sebastian Fry still did not respond.

"What's wrong, my friend?" asked Aidan, this time with more sensitivity.

The little elf turned his head slightly, although still not looking at Aidan.

'I'm hopefull that the prophecy
Is true, but it's too late for me'

"What do you mean *it's too late for you*?" asked Aidan. Sebastian turned to walk away, but Aidan stopped him and bid him to sit back down at the table.

'Questions will not help you now
But one can hope and pray
The future is what matters most
The past has gone away'

"Sebastian!" insisted Aidan. "I've been told to ask questions. Please tell me what you're talking about. How has the past gone away?"

The little elf wiped a tear from his cheek.

Aidan of Oren

'Seven years, and endless tears
Have crossed the hands of time
Since I held Mathias
The only son of mine
A quiet night, so innocent
He was the very first
Until, alas, more disappeared
To feed the Shadow's thirst'

"No!" gasped Aidan, not knowing what else to say. He leaned over to hug the now weeping Sebastian Fry. "No!" he gasped again. He closed his eyes as his face wrenched with pain. The young boy's heart was torn between anger and compassion. How could this happen? Not to Sebastian! Not to any of these precious people!

"NO!" GASPED AIDAN

Frederick the Juggler

Aidan could feel that the wind had started blowing quite hard. He opened his eyes to see that the sky had darkened. Those sitting around the table had become silent. All that were seated, including Lira, Lilly and McKenzie, were staring at him. Horribly embarrassed, and still very upset, Aidan quickly left the table and entered the woods behind the library where he could be alone to think. Seating himself on a tree stump, Aidan turned his back to the others. He could hear them whispering, and his imagination started getting the best of him as he wondered what they could be saying.

The crackling of twigs caught his attention. Someone was coming. He turned his head toward the library and saw that an elf was coming up the path. It was Frederick. The shy little elf walked up to Aidan and patted him on the knee.

'Don't be sad, and don't be shy
You called the wind down from the sky
Your heart was touched, and you displayed
Something special on this day
Please be our guest, please take your place
And let a smile ring on your face
As for me, it's time to go
My home is far away, you know'

Aidan, wiping a tear away from his own eye, was astonished at the maturity of this small elf.

"How can you be calm?" Aidan asked. "Aren't you afraid of the Shadow? Are children still disappearing?"

'Reality is what you see
Fear is not our rule

We simply go inside our homes
When the daylight starts to cool'
"But, for seven years? How can the elves bear such a curse?"
'We choose a path of happiness
Regardless of the curse
Day by day we celebrate
By singing of a verse
A verse that tells a winding tale
Of one that soon will come
Who holds the hope of everyone
To fill the Shadow with the sun'
"There it is again . . . that statement!" exclaimed Aidan. "Does that refer to me?"

Little Frederick just shrugged his shoulders.

"The food's almost gone!" came a familiar voice from behind him. Aidan turned to see McKenzie waving from the table, trying to get his attention. "Come on, Aidan, don't spoil the party. We're waiting for you!"

Frederick jumped down from Aidan's knee and started walking away.

"Hey! I've got a few more questions for you!" shouted Aidan after him. Frederick called back to him.

'You know I'd really like to stay
But the daylight soon will go away'

The little elf turned and started running down the path. Just then, Aidan noticed movement over by the Library. As he focused his eyes on the lower corner of the building, he could faintly see a window with iron bars. He rubbed his eyes in disbelief as he realized what else he saw. The creature from the library was standing behind the window in what must have been a lower portion of the building, reaching through the bars as he watched Frederick scurry down the path. The creature appeared to desperately want to get to the little elf, but the bars held fast. Suddenly, the creature turned its attention to Aidan and they locked eyes. The creature slowly pulled its arms back inside the building and slipped into the darkness.

Aidan took a few steps back toward the tables where everyone else was eating, afraid to take his eyes off of the building. He tripped on a tree root, almost losing his balance, then turned and hurried out of the woods.

CHAPTER 9

Flying Rocks

idan quickly seated himself back beside the table. He was still shaken by what he had seen. The creature called Elijah was obviously dangerous, and he couldn't understand how Noam could befriend such a beast. Noam seemed to be wise in many ways, but this didn't make sense.

"Aidan!" Lilly interrupted his thoughts. "I think the feast is about over. The elves are starting to leave."

"I don't want it to end," said McKenzie. "This has been the best day of my whole life!"

Sebastian Fry stood to his feet.

The day is drawing to an end
Please come and follow me
A place has been prepared for you
Beside the Sycamore tree'

"Sebastian," said Aidan softly. "I'm sorry if I embarrassed you. I just didn't know . . ."

Sebastian Fry took Aidan's hand.

'You did nothing wrong, my friend
In fact, you showed concern
And so, I wish to thank you

Flying Rocks

Because, for me, you burn'

"I just can't believe . . ."

The little elf turned and started leading Aidan away.

"Aidan," said Lilly. "Sebastian told us about his son, Mathias. It's so very sad, but we must move on. I know he appreciates your concern. But as leader, his job now is to consider the safety of everyone else . . . including us."

Aidan nodded without saying a word as the three children, Charles and Damon, were led to an old elf house that sat beside a large Sycamore tree. It was larger than the other elf houses they had seen along the way. This was a good thing, as the three of them would have never fit comfortably inside a normal elf house.

Upon entering the abode, Sebastian Fry placed a large candle on a solitary table in the middle of the room. The table, which was surrounded by three chairs, was very old, but quite solid. The small elf leader was quiet, but steadfast in purpose as he lit the candle and turned around.

'Darkness falls in just a bit
Be sure to keep the candle lit'

The children looked at each other, not knowing what to say. Sebastian bowed slightly then quickly departed. As darkness engulfed the valley, each of the children prepared themselves for the evening. They soon gathered around the table in the middle of the room to talk about the events of the day. Damon yawned, then pitter pattered his way over beside one of the beds where he hunched over for a good night's sleep.

"He seems pretty tired," chuckled Aidan. No one said a word. "He doesn't seem too worried about the Shadow, does he?" A great feeling of uneasiness filled the room. "I guess we had better keep the candle lit, huh?"

"Hmph!" snorted Charles. "I don't believe in this Shadow business. I think our little friends are a bit superstitious!"

"Don't be so sure," said Aidan. "We've seen some pretty strange things since we've been here . . ."

"Oh, grow up, Aidan! In the first place, no one's ever seen this *Shadow*. And, if no one's ever seen it, how can they name it?"

"I believe Sebastian Fry," said Aidan, a little perturbed. "Did you forget that seven years ago he lost his son? And, ever since, children have continued to disappear? Something very bad is happening here. Something is taking the children."

"Oh, right . . . and, this candle is supposed to *protect* us?"

"I think Charles has a point," interrupted McKenzie as she stood up and leaned over the table. "I'll just blow out the candle so we can all get a good sleep . . ."

"No!" screeched Charles. "The Shadow!" A deadening silence filled the room as Charles ruffled his feathers in embarrassment. "Oh . . . um, I was just trying to . . . protect you . . . oh, hmph!" snorted Charles again. "You're not funny!"

"Aidan," said McKenzie softly as she sat back down in her seat. "Wait 'till I tell you what I saw today! I was taken to the place where rocks take flight . . ."

Flying Rocks

"Excuse me," said Charles all-knowingly. "Rocks do not have wings, and therefore certainly cannot fly."

"Sure they can," said McKenzie confidently. "I saw them, and so did Frederick and Sprite!"

"That reminds me," said Aidan. "About Frederick, I saw something earlier that I've been wondering about . . ."

"Tell me, then," interrupted Charles as he continued his bantering with McKenzie. "Exactly how do rocks take flight when they have no wings?"

"Well," said McKenzie slowly as the candle flickered. "There's a cliff that rises out of the earth. It's so high it seems to reach for the sky. I was taken to the top of a hill not far from here, which has the best view of the cliff. Against the clear blue sky of day, you could see rocks leaping, one every little while, out into the sky where they would fly. They would fly all the way to the ground."

"That's not flying," quipped Charles. "That's *falling*! The cliff is obviously unstable and crumbling . . ."

"No," said McKenzie mysteriously as the candlelight danced across her eyes. "They were *flying*."

CHAPTER 10

The Arboree

I believe you," said Lilly softly. "After what I saw today, I'd believe just about anything."

"What do you mean?" asked Aidan. "You went to the Arboree, didn't you? I would think that you would have seen lots of trees . . ."

"Oh, my yes! But, they weren't just any kind of trees. They were the largest I've ever seen! The tops of them were so high and so thick, you could not see the sun from inside! Sebastian Fry said that the treetops have grown together so that it never rains within the boundaries of the trees. You can't go very far into the Arboree, though, because it gets very dark. However, the outer rim is absolutely beautiful!" Lilly paused. "But . . ."

"What is it?" asked Aidan. "You seem bothered by something."

"Oh, no, here we go again," sighed Charles. "Don't tell me . . . you saw a monster. Am I right?"

Lilly looked startled. "How . . . how did you know?"

"Oh, please don't start playing this game! Nothing is ever simple with the three of you! I'm not hearing any more of it!" The perturbed falcon jumped to the ground and waddled over to where Damon was sleeping and wedged his way between the baby dragon and a feather pillow that lay on the floor. Once settled, the children could faintly hear him muffle, "now leave me alone!"

"Oh, Lilly," laughed McKenzie. "You're better at teasing Charles than I am!"

"If only I were teasing . . ."

"Hey!" Aidan jumped into the conversation. "Just what did you see?"

McKenzie's eyes widened with expectation. Lilly pulled her hair back and tucked it behind her ears, leaned across the table, and started talking in a hushed voice. She was speaking so quickly and quietly that the others could hardly tell what she was saying. "Louder, Lilly, I can't hear you!" whined McKenzie. "There's nobody here except for us!"

Lilly slowly turned to face McKenzie. "Don't be so sure."

"Alright," said Aidan. "Let's not panic. Did I hear you say that you saw something in the Arboree?"

"Well," Lilly started again, this time a bit more controlled. "I'm not sure what I saw . . . I only know what I think I saw." Aidan and McKenzie wrinkled their noses in confusion. Lilly laughed nervously. "I guess that didn't sound quite right. But, I did see something deep in the Arboree. I was admiring the canopy formed by the tops of the trees, and wondering just how dark it must be deeper into the woods, when . . . when I saw something move."

"What was it?" asked McKenzie, hardly able to contain herself. "What did you see?"

Lilly stared across the candle toward her friends, studying their faces as if she was afraid they might not believe her.

"It's alright," said Aidan. "Just tell us what you think you saw."

"I saw someone, or something, behind one of the very large trees deep into the Arboree. And, it saw me . . ."

"What saw you?" asked McKenzie impatiently.

"A person, I think, but with a hideous face and long, scary arms . . ."

"Did it try to eat you?"

"No," Lilly laughed a little. "It couldn't get to me because it was growing out of the ground . . . just like a tree."

"Are you sure of this?" gasped Aidan. "I've never heard of such a thing!"

"As I said, this is what I *think* I saw. Before I could get a better look, Walter pulled me back from the edge of the forest. He told me that the Arboree was beautiful to visit, but no one is permitted to enter. And, he told me that it was forbidden to look into the dark places. He said that there are creatures that live deep inside the forest . . . creatures that are dangerous and misshapen. When I told him that I saw something moving, yet rooted in the ground, he simply took my hand and led me away. He wouldn't speak of it again. So, you see, I'm not sure . . ."

The Arboree

"What a day this has been," sighed Aidan. "There is much to this land that we do not understand. But, we're here to learn, at least that's what Grandmama told me."

"I think we're here to help," said McKenzie as she looked out one of the windows of the cottage. "The stars sure are bright tonight."

"I don't know how we can help," said Aidan. "All I know is that I'm a student, and that I have a very strange and unusual mouse as a teacher."

"You both may be right," added Lilly. "I think, yes

. . . you may both be right. Aidan, you said something earlier about little Frederick. You had a concern?"

Aidan proceeded to tell the two girls about his adventure with Noam and the chest that would someday belong to his Grandmama. He described Elijah, the beast in the library, in great detail, much to the amusement of McKenzie. He told them of his conversation with little Frederick, and how he spotted Elijah watching Frederick very closely, even trying to get to him, as the elf child walked away.

"Oooh," said Lilly as she started rubbing her eyes. "It sounds like you've had the strangest day of all, Aidan!"

"I don't know," he mused, winking at McKenzie. "Flying rocks seem pretty strange as well."

"That's not all that was strange," said McKenzie. "You remember Olivia, the tall stranger we met this morning? Well, she didn't seem to care for the flying rocks at all. She just stared over the hill down into the valley."

"That's where we were!" exclaimed Lilly. "We were in the valley! I wonder what she was looking at?"

"I didn't see her at the feast," said Aidan. "Didn't she come back with you, McKenzie?"

"No," she said, shaking her head from side to side. "She said she had some things to do, and that she would see us later."

CRACKK!

"What was that?" said Aidan as he jumped to his feet.

The Arboree

Lilly ran over to the window on the south side of the little building and looked out. "I see something moving in the darkness!"

Aidan ran to the door and started to open it when it stopped with a thud. He looked down to see Damon standing steadfastly in front of the door.

"What are you doing?" he shouted. "There's something out there!"

The little dragon, which had been so quiet ever since they had arrived in the valley of the elves, nodded his head. "Uh, huh, there's something out there. That's why you have to stay in here."

"Don't be silly!" insisted Aidan. "Let me pass!"

Damon would not move. Aidan leaned down and tried to push him out of the way, but the little dragon would not budge. Then, Aidan reached behind Damon and grabbed his tail, attempting to drag him out of the way, but still to no avail. As Aidan pulled with all of his might, his hands slipped off of Damon's tail, sending him tumbling backwards where he hit his head on the floor.

"Damon!" shouted Aidan, now so frustrated his eyes were beginning to tear up. "You're supposed to listen to me!"

The baby dragon lovingly looked over to his young master. "No. I'm supposed to *protect* you."

CHAPTER 11

Whispers

hat do you mean, you're supposed to protect me?" asked Aidan, now rubbing the spot where a large bump was forming on his head.

"There's danger," said Damon. "Uh, I've heard whispers. Whispers in the wind."

"That's right!" Aidan stood up and approached the little dragon. "You can speak any language, can't you? What are the elves saying?"

"Not the elves," said Damon as he turned away. He headed back over to the soft pillow on the floor where Charles was trying desperately to sleep.

"Not the elves?" asked Aidan and Lilly together.

Damon turned around. "Not the elves. The whispers are bad."

"What's wrong with your face?" asked McKenzie. Aidan and Lilly took a step back. Something was different. The countenance of the baby dragon, normally innocent and playful, was changing. His eyes narrowed and his forehead seemed to tighten, giving him an almost ferocious appearance. He gazed at the children for a moment, and then retreated toward his sleeping area in the corner of the cottage. Charles, who had opened one eye to see what was going on, quickly scurried under Aidan's bed as Damon approached the pillow. The baby dragon hunched down and gave a heavy sigh, a sign that it was time to sleep.

"Wait," urged Aidan. "I hear voices in the wind, too. But I didn't hear anything bad . . ."

Damon seemed a little perturbed. "You can't hear it. You hear only good."

"Why? Why can I hear only good? Tell me . . ."

The little dragon's voice deepened, and bore a hint of an echo. "Because you *are* good."

Aidan paused. "Then, why can you hear evil?"

"I don't know," replied Damon, now turning his back toward the children and lowering his head to sleep. "I don't know."

"Your voice . . . what's happening to you, Damon?"

Lilly grabbed Aidan's arm and gave him the type of look that told him the discussion was over. McKenzie put a single finger over her lips, motioning for Aidan to be quiet. They sat around the candle for what seemed like a very long time, waiting for Damon to fall asleep. Finally, the little dragon began to snore loudly. But this time it wasn't funny.

Lilly took Aidan's hand. "We really don't know anything about dragons, do we?"

"I won't hear it!" protested McKenzie in a loud whisper. "Damon is good! He's our friend!"

"Now, hold on a moment," Lilly cautioned. "Remember how Noam seemed almost afraid of Damon? Didn't that seem a bit strange? Aidan, do you remember Grandmama's stories about the dragons?"

"Well . . ."

"I do!" blurted in McKenzie. "They are magnificent creatures!"

Aidan started talking again. "I think . . ."

"Yes," added Lilly. "But they are also extremely dangerous. We should not take anything for granted with our little friend."

"Can I *please* say something?" asked Aidan, trying desperately to get into the conversation. Lilly and McKenzie stopped talking and looked at him blankly. "I remember the stories alright, but this is different. Dragon's are normally red . . . but Damon's a white dragon. White means that he's good, right?"

"We should not presume anything," said Lilly. "He

could hear evil speaking in the wind, how is that possible?"

The candle flickered, and there was a moment of silence.

"He speaks any language, remember?" argued McKenzie. "He's just tired, that's all. He'll be fine in the morning."

Aidan stood up and helped the girls to their feet. "I think we need to get to sleep, too. I have no idea what tomorrow will bring."

"I do!" squealed McKenzie as she hopped on to her straw mattress. "Sebastian Fry and Frederick are going to take Lilly and I to the Haven, where we will be witness to a very ancient custom of story telling . . . a ritual that *always* happens on the second day of The Elf Princess' visit."

"I thought she didn't visit very often."

"She doesn't, silly. But when she does, there are certain events that take place as part of their heritage, which dates back a very long time. For example, on the first day of her visit, a great feast is prepared. Then . . ."

"I know, McKenzie, I was there. So, what else happens during her visit?"

"Well, if you would please let me finish, I'll tell you. The second day is called the Day of Stories, which to the elves is like sharing gifts. The entire community gathers together, young and old alike. The elders go first, spinning tales throughout the morning. The Elf Princess then returns the favor in the afternoon . . . it is said that she tells the most wonderful stories. Lilly and I don't want to miss one word!"

"That sounds pretty interesting. I'd like to . . ."

"I'm not finished," she interrupted. "The third day is called the Day of Song. It is a day of celebration and harmony. I can't wait for that." There was a moment of silence as Aidan peered over at McKenzie, not quite sure if he should talk. "Alright, I'm done!" she giggled.

"Well," said Aidan, now laying back into his own bed. "It sounds like your day will be very interesting indeed. I wonder what I will be doing."

"I heard Sebastian Fry say that you would be taking a trip with Noam to see someone," said Lilly.

"Hmmm . . . who could that be?" mused Aidan. "Another mouse creature? Oh, my, I hope I don't have to meet Elijah again . . . what a beast he was! Or, maybe . . ."

"Don't worry about it," said Lilly comfortingly. "Things will look clearer tomorrow."

"Yeah," chimed in McKenzie. "Tomorrow's always a good day, isn't it?"

Aidan laughed. "Yes, tomorrow's all about hope."

"And dreams . . ." said Lilly mysteriously.

Aidan turned to look over at her, but she was already asleep. "Did you hear that, McKenzie?" he asked. But to his amazement, McKenzie was also fast asleep. He rolled over in his bed, staring at the ceiling, where he, too, drifted off into a deep, deep sleep.

CHAPTER 12

Aidan's Nightmare

No! Nooo!" Aidan screamed as he awoke with a start.

"What's wrong?" asked McKenzie as she rushed over to his bed. "Why are you screaming?" Aidan sat straight up, he was breathing hard and his eyes were wild with fear. He rubbed his arms, chest and neck frantically. McKenzie grabbed his face and looked him in the eyes. "It's alright, Aidan. You were just dreaming. It's morning, now. Don't be afraid!"

Aidan stared back into his little friend's eyes. His breathing slowed as he realized that it was, after all, only a dream.

"*Oh, my goodness!*" screeched Charles, crawling out from under the bed. "What on earth is all the commotion about? I was finally getting some badly needed rest. I do not appreciate being disturbed!"

Aidan didn't say a word. He reached out and hugged McKenzie, shooting an angry glance down to Charles from over her shoulder.

"What did I do?" asked Charles indignantly. "I'm not the one making all of the noise!"

Aidan of Oren

Aidan turned to see Lilly behind them, quietly making her bed. She glanced a look of reassurance in his direction. Suddenly, a shuffling sound turned their attention toward the corner of the room. Damon, still hunched with his back to the children, was starting to awaken. Aidan wondered if his face would retain the same dark appearance that it had taken on the night before. All three children, not to mention Charles, held their breath as the little dragon slowly turned around. Damon yawned, and started wiping his eyes with his little hands, which kept everyone from clearly seeing his face.

Charles, getting impatient with Damon's antics, could take no more. "Oh, would you please stop all of that rubbing and yawning! *Look at us*, you infantile beast!"

"I'm hungry," said Damon as he stopped rubbing his eyes and looked at his friends. Each of them breathed a sigh of relief as they could see that Damon was back to normal. The frightening countenance from the night before was gone, and his soft, rounded voice had returned to normal. Aidan laughed out loud and walked over to pat Damon on his head. "It's good to see you're back with us, my friend. I'm sure a good breakfast is waiting for all of us!"

"One would certainly *hope* so!" crooned Charles. "It's the least they could do for stuffing us into this tiny building. Why, I think some nuts roasted over the fire would be a fine choice, don't you?"

Aidan's Nightmare

"No!" gasped Aidan in horror, clutching his chest and backing up to sit on his bed. "Not the fire!"

"Lilly!" shouted McKenzie as she sat down with Aidan. "Something's wrong! Come help!"

Lilly calmly finished making her bed and pulled up a chair so she could sit in front of Aidan, who sat speechless on the side of his bed. She glanced over to McKenzie. "He had a dream," she said. "In fact, he's been having a lot of dreams, haven't you, Aidan?"

Aidan nodded. "How did you know?"

Lilly laughed. "Because I hear you talking in your sleep. Last night you seemed very upset . . ."

"Why didn't you awaken me?"

"Because dreams are nature's way of working out problems. Sometimes there are messages in the dreams that guide us, and sometimes the dream is simply a way to relieve pressures we may be keeping inside of us."

"No!" shouted Aidan. "This was not a dream . . . it was a *nightmare*. I've had my share of dreams, but this was an absolute horror! It served no purpose other than to scare me to death!"

"Even in nightmares, there are lessons," chided Lilly. Her tone softened. "Tell us what you saw."

"Yes!" squealed McKenzie. "Tell us all about it, and don't leave out any of the scary stuff!"

Aidan ruffled McKenzie's hair, and noticed that Lilly had that mysterious look on her face again. So, he cleared his throat and tried to be more serious.

"I dreamed that I was walking through a forest. It

was at night, I think, because it was very dark. I heard voices of what sounded like many, many children. The voices seemed to be all around me, calling my name. I looked all around, but could see only the shadows of trees. A game, I thought, so I started to run . . . faster and faster, I looked behind every tree I came to, but no one was there. Then, I heard another voice . . . a familiar voice." Aidan stopped and looked down at Damon, who had come up and rested his chin on Aidan's knee. The little dragon was listening intently, as were the girls. Even Charles was spellbound.

"Who's voice was it?" asked McKenzie. "C'mon, don't leave us in suspense!"

"Just as I turned toward the voice, I was engulfed by fire."

"Fire!" gasped Lilly and McKenzie together.

"Not just any fire . . . this fire was the breath of a dragon. I looked down at my arms and my legs . . . I tried to scream, but couldn't, as I could see my skin melting down to the bone. I saw myself burning alive."

Silence filled the room. No one dared say a word. Aidan forced a smile as his words began to break up. "The voice I heard . . . it was Damon."

"No," said McKenzie in a hushed whisper.

"Yes," said Aidan emphatically. "But it was just a dream."

Damon's eyes pointed up at Aidan as the little dragon smiled.

Aidan's Nightmare

"You would never breathe fire on me, now would you my little friend?" said Aidan nervously as he patted the little dragon on the head. Damon continued to smile at Aidan, but said nothing.

CHAPTER 13

The Scribe's Cottage

t's time to go
Let's not be slow!'

A voice boomed in from the doorway. It was Sebastian Fry, seemingly bright and refreshed from a good night's sleep. He took Lilly and McKenzie by the hand and started to lead them out the door.

'Much to do, this sunny day
Much to see, come right this way
Aidan, Damon, Charles, too
Noam awaits the three of you'

The little elf stopped suddenly at the door. He let go of the hands he was holding and rubbed the wooden door that now stood open.

'Scratches are upon your door
Scratches deep down to the core
Did you hear a sound last night?
Did you keep the candle bright?'

"Yes!" Exclaimed Aidan. "We did hear a sound, even though the candle was lit. I tried to go see what it was, but Damon stopped me!"

The leader of the elves looked worried.

The Scribe's Cottage

'The dragon may have saved your life
The Shadow's claws cut like a knife
The candle did not keep away
A bolder Shadow's here to stay'

"Sebastian, whom is Noam taking me to see today? McKenzie said . . ." The leader of the elves walked up and put his little hand over Aidan's mouth.

'Nothing spoken, nothing heard
I do not know, but rest assured
If the teacher teaches as teachers can
Trust the teacher's final plan'

The little elf turned, again took Lilly and McKenzie by the hand, and proceeded to lead them back to the elf village.

"Oh, *that* made a lot of sense!" quipped Charles. "I do believe our little friend has lost a few of his marbles . . ."

"Charles!" snapped Aidan. "That's no way to talk about our host. He's been very kind to us, so you need to show a little respect, don't you think?"

Not wanting to listen to any more scolding, the red falcon puffed out his chest and buried his beak into his back wings. Aidan just shook his head and made final preparations to leave. Nothing more was said as he placed Charles on his shoulder and left the little cottage. As he closed the wooden door, he ran his hand over the scratches that were not there the day before. They were deep and jagged. Maybe Damon was right to keep him inside after all. He reached down and patted his little dragon friend on the head. "Thank you," he said softly. "I don't know what made these marks, but it certainly does seem that you have protected me." He turned and started walking down the path toward the elf village. Damon followed close behind, softly cooing and apparently in a very good mood.

The winding path took them along the edge of a large wooded area. It was a quiet morning, quieter still given the fact that Charles was pouting. Aidan stopped suddenly, which prompted Charles to pull his head out of his back feathers. "What's wrong?" he demanded. "Why did you stop here?"

"Shhh!" hushed Aidan with his finger across his lips. "I hear something, it's coming from in the woods!"

"No!" shouted Charles. "Keep walking . . . whatever you do, *please* do not take me in there!"

Aidan gently lowered Charles to the ground beside Damon. "The two of you stay here, I'll be right back . . ."

"Oh, good idea, Aidan," said Charles nervously as he began to step backward toward the little cottage where they slept. "You go on ahead . . . yes, we'll just wait here . . ." Damon nodded and sat down, right on Charles' tail. "Excuse me!" shouted the irritated falcon. "Get off of my tail, you giant clumsy baby!"

Damon would not move, and so it seemed Charles was hopelessly pinned. That was Aidan's cue to head into the woods. He heard a soft crackling of branches ahead of him and quietly moved forward, where he soon spotted a very small cottage. His senses were tingling as he moved closer for a better look. The cottage appeared empty. He reached the doorway, where he had to lean down to walk inside. There, he noticed yellowish scrolls scattered all through the cottage. A small table was turned over. Beside it, a lifeless candle lay on the floor. The hair stood up on the back of his neck as he noticed large, jagged scratches on the walls, the floor, even across the overturned table. "What happened here?" he gasped as he covered his mouth with his hand.

A soft female voice caught his attention as he exited the rear of the cottage. He turned to his left and noticed that someone was standing behind a large tree out in the courtyard. He froze, listening, not wanting to be heard. All he could see were two, delicate, trembling hands holding part of a scroll. The mysterious girl was speaking softly in verses, too softly for Aidan to understand what was being said. The verses were repeated over and over again and again, and then the girl stopped, seemingly too overcome with emotion to say any more. She began to sob softly. In that same moment, rain began to fall. Aidan stood silently, deeply moved by this experience.

"This must be Lira," he thought. "How do I approach her? What would I say?" Aidan gathered his nerve and stepped around the tree to greet her, but stopped abruptly when he saw that it was not the Elf Princess after all.

"Olivia!" he gasped. "What are you doing here? Why are you holding that paper in your hands?"

"Hello, Aidan," she said mysteriously. "Something bad has happened here. Judging from all of the scrolls scattered about, it appears that the elf who lived here was a scribe."

"But ..." Aidan was trying to catch his breath. "What happened to him? And what is that you're holding in your hand?"

Olivia did not answer directly. She held up the piece of torn parchment in her hands. "I think it's ..."

She was interrupted as Aidan reached over and took the paper for himself. "Hmm, I can't read this ... it's written in Elf! From the looks of things he was either a sloppy writer or in a very big hurry ..."

"Maybe I can help," said Olivia as she took back the parchment. "I can read Elf, you know."

"Really," asked Aidan suspiciously. "What does it say then?"

Olivia held out the paper in front of her, but there was a distant look in her eyes as she read:

'Age to age and fire to fire
Hearts arise and dreams inspire
When life and death become as one
The Shadow's reign has just begun
Until one soars where eagles fly
And brings the fire from the sky
Then the reign of darkness ends
Then the hearts of all shall mend'

Quietly, she knelt down beside Aidan. She laid the tattered scroll on the ground and dug a small hole in the dirt. Then, she repeated what she had just read as she placed the little scroll in the hole and gently covered it with dirt. Aidan could be silent no longer.

"What are you doing?" he asked.

"Planting a seed," she said as she gently patted the dirt. "I'm planting a seed."

AGE to AGE and FIRE to FIRE HEARTS ARISE and DREAMS INSPIRE....

She held up the torn parchment in her hand.

CHAPTER 14

Frederick Disappears

I must go," said Olivia as she turned toward the deep forest.

"Wait, I'd like to ask you about . . ."

They were interrupted by a distant cry from Charles. "Aidan! Aidan! *Where are you?* I believe this beast may be doing permanent damage to my feathers!"

Aidan turned to go, then turned back toward the Olivia. "Oh, my friends! I forgot all about them. Before I go, I do have one question."

"Ask whatever you want, Aidan of Oren."

"How is it that you can read the Elf language?" The question seemed to make Olivia nervous. "You don't look much older than I am," said Aidan awkwardly. "Just how old are you?"

Olivia laughed. "How old are you, Aidan of Oren?"

"I'm thirteen."

"Let's just say that I'm older than you. Go, Aidan. Go to your friends and be on your way."

"Aidan!" The cry from Charles was deafening. "Would you *please* hurry? I'm getting a cramp!"

Frederick Disappears

Aidan grimaced in embarrassment. "He's somewhat of a complainer, that one . . ."

Before he could finish, Olivia had retreated deeper into the woods. "Goodbye, Aidan," she said, her voice fainting in the distance. "I'm sure that we'll see each other again very soon."

Aidan watched her walk away. Something didn't seem quite right, but there was no time to think any more about it. Charles was getting a cramp.

"Oh, heavens!" cried Charles as Aidan stepped out of the woods. "It's about time! Please remove your clumsy dragon from my hind quarters!"

Damon laughed softly as if he had thoroughly enjoyed his sit down time with Charles. Aidan did not hear the laughter, however, his mind was still trying to figure out what had just happened back in the woods. The three of them traveled to the elf village without much discussion, where they soon stood before the stone building called the Hall of Judges; Noam's home. They walked up to the front door and noticed that it was already slightly open.

Charles took that very opportunity to jump off of Aidan's shoulder to the ground. "You'll excuse me if I just wait out here on the steps, won't you?"

Aidan shot him a sarcastic look.

Charles simply ruffled his feathers. "What? Are you surprised that I don't want to be eaten?"

"I'm hungry," said Damon, which prompted a dirty look from Charles.

"Don't even *think* about it," the falcon sneered.

Just then, three little elves walked up to Aidan, Damon and Charles, where they placed a tray of fruit and cheese in front of each of them.

"Oh, now *that's* what I'm talking about!" shouted Charles gleefully as all three of them began to eat. After quickly devouring a few pieces of cheese and an apple,

Aidan walked up to the top of the steps toward the open door. He stuck his head inside the library. "Noam? Noam? Are you home?"

"Oh, *please*," sighed Charles. "You're starting to sound like one of *them*!"

Aidan pulled his head back out of the building and looked blankly at the falcon.

"You know, the whole rhyming thing . . . you just did it!"

Aidan, realizing that he had talked in a rhyme, started laughing. "You're right, I did . . ."

Frederick Disappears

The clanking sound of a hammer against metal interrupted his laughter. It was coming from behind the stone building. "Charles, do you want to come with me to see what's making that noise?"

The red falcon lazily stretched his wings in the warm sun and replied, "actually, I think I'll sit this one out. Just leave Damon with me."

"Alright, but he might still be hungry . . ."

"Oh, stop it! Why does everyone think they're so funny today?"

Aidan laughed, then walked around to the back of the building to see what was making the noise. To his amazement, he found Noam hammering a set of iron bars onto one of the lower level windows.

"Noam?" asked Aidan. "What's going on? Aren't we supposed to meet someone today?"

The curious mouse turned around. His little arms were fidgeting, and he seemed very nervous. "Oh, yes. Yes, today we are supposed to travel into the lower valley. Yes . . ."

"What are you doing?" asked Aidan. "I thought those bars were attached yesterday . . . I was back here during part of the banquet. I saw the creature . . ."

"Elijah! Yes, I'm putting the bars back on because . . . because Elijah got out last night. I don't like it when he does this. No, I don't like it at all . . ."

"You mean this isn't the first time he's broken out?" asked Aidan as concern welled inside of him.

"No," said Noam, who now seemed completely exasperated. "Once in a while he gets out. Different ways, really. He's very smart, you know ... yes, very smart and very strong." Noam was so nervous that he had difficulty holding the bars steady so they could be nailed.

"Would you like some help?" said Aidan as he motioned for the hammer.

Noam reluctantly handed over the hammer and a few crude iron nails. "Thank you," is all he said as Aidan secured the remaining iron bars to the window.

Noam's display of insecurity was quite different from what Aidan had seen the day before. Today Noam seemed almost fragile, not to mention extremely over protective of the creature he kept chained within the stone building.

Sprite walked up from behind, startling them both.

'I hate to bother you this way
But Frederick's not here today

Frederick Disappears

I've also heard the elders say
The scribe is gone ... taken away'

"Oh, that's not good," said Noam, nervously patting his hands together. He quickly gathered up the tools and headed back to the front of the building. "We must hurry, Aidan. Time is short . . . yes, very short!"

CHAPTER 15

Three Blue Stones

idan knelt down beside Sprite, who looked very sad. "What do you mean, Frederick's not here today?"

Sprite wiped away a little tear.

'**He never misses morning play**
He's always here at break of day
Just a child full of vim
The Shadow may have come for him'

Aidan thought back to the day before. He remembered how the creature, Elijah, had tried desperately to reach through the bars toward Frederick. He escaped sometime during the night, and now little Frederick was missing. Aidan bounded up the steps of the Hall of Judges, passing Damon and Charles without saying a word. Charles all but ignored the commotion, but Damon followed Aidan inside.

"Noam!" he shouted. "Noam, where are you?"

The door was open enough for him to see most of library, although it was still dark in the corners. Damon shuffled to the center of the room and sat down by the dragon chest. "What's this?" he asked.

Three Blue Stones

"You scared me!" exclaimed Aidan as he quickly turned around. He had not seen Damon enter the room. "Oh, the chest. That's something Noam has been working on for a while . . ."

"Two dragons."

Aidan could see that Damon was very interested in the carvings on the side of the chest. He walked over beside his little friend and pointed to the black and white carvings. "Yes, there are two dragons."

"Uh, huh. One white dragon," Damon paused and looked down at himself. "And one black dragon." He looked up at Aidan. "Who's the black dragon?"

"I don't know. I'm not sure what the symbols mean."

Damon looked at the chest again. "They're fighting."

"Well, yes, they do appear to be fighting. But, I've really never asked what the symbols mean . . ."

Their conversation was interrupted by the sound of an iron chain. They both turned to see something moving behind one of the bookcases. "One moment, please . . ." It was Noam's voice.

"Noam, what are you doing back there?" asked Aidan.

"Oh, a question!" said the mouse as he led the creature out from behind the bookcase. "I'm just chaining Elijah down. Don't want him to get out again. No . . . we don't want that."

Elijah was breathing hard. He made eye contact with Aidan and quickly looked away. Then his eyes fixated on Damon sitting in the middle of the room. He opened his mouth, revealing the horrific razor like teeth inside, and let out a deep growl which seemed to shake the floor."

"Elijah!" shouted Noam. "No!"

The creature did not respond to his master's command. Rather, he took a step toward the baby dragon. Though the lighting was dim, Aidan could see Damon's eyes narrow and his forehead pull back. This was the same look the children had seen the night before. He looked almost as ferocious as Elijah. Suddenly, two small flames could be seen ever so briefly from the Dragon's nostrils, and the room immediately filled with smoke.

"No, no, no!" shrieked Noam, rushing toward Damon. He took the baby dragon by the shoulders and moved him quickly toward the front door, which was still open. Luckily, Damon offered no resistance. "No smoking in the building!" gasped Noam, now out of breath, as he pushed Damon outside.

Aidan's attention was drawn to the creature. It seemed to be clutching something in its right hand.

"What do you have there?" he asked.

The creature seemed frightened by the question and backed up a couple of steps.

Noam rejoined them. "We will be on our way as soon as I finish taking care of Elijah. Do you want to wait outside?"

"No," Aidan swallowed hard. "But I would like to see what Elijah has in his right hand."

Again, the creature took a step back.

Noam gestured toward the creature. "What do you have, Elijah. Come now. Easy . . . show us what you have."

The creature reluctantly opened his right hand, revealing three peculiar blue stones.

"Hey!" shouted Aidan. "I've seen those before. They belong to Frederick!"

The creature seemed to groan as if in pain. "FRE . . . D . . . K!"

"He talked!" Noam said, greatly surprised. "That's the first time, yes, the very first time I've ever heard him say anything!"

"He said Frederick!" shouted Aidan. "And those are Frederick's stones he uses to juggle with!" Aidan quickly grabbed the three stones out of the creature's hand. It did not try to resist. Instead, Elijah tried again to speak. "FRE . . . D . . . K! FRED . . . R . . . IK!"

"Hmmm . . ." mused Noam as he finished securing the heavy, iron shackles to the creature. "So very interesting."

"What does that mean?" asked Aidan as he tucked the three little stones into his leather pouch. Noam ignored him. The mouse teacher walked to the center of the room where the Dragon Chest lay open on the table. Looking up toward the hole in the ceiling, Noam squinted at the ray of light illuminating the chest. Nodding slightly, displaying some kind of mysterious approval, he closed the chest and patted it on top, whispering softly, "soon . . . soon".

Noam headed for the open door. "Let's be on our way now, no time . . . no time to waste!"

"Wait!" cried Aidan. He caught up with Noam just outside the great wooden door, which was now being closed and locked. As Noam turned around, Aidan stopped him. "I have another question. Is it possible that the creature has something to do with Frederick being missing . . . and the scribe as well?"

Noam's nose started twitching wildly. "He has a name, Aidan. He couldn't hurt anybody . . . he's from the line of Cuchulainn."

"*Think about it!*" persisted Aidan. "He had Frederick's juggling stones. Doesn't that seem a little strange to you? As for the line of Cuchulainn, isn't it possible that something evil could come from something good?"

Three Blue Stones

This question made Noam stop what he was doing. For once, he wasn't trembling. For once, his nose wasn't twitching wildly.

"That's a *good* question," said the mouse soberly. "Let's look at it another way, Aidan. Yes, let's ask another question. Can something good come from something evil?"

Aidan wanted to say yes, but even he had doubts that any good could come from evil. Without saying another word, Noam turned and headed down a winding path. Aidan quickly gathered Charles and went after him, with Damon following close behind.

CHAPTER 16

The Forgotten Castle

here in blazes we going?" asked Charles once he caught his breath. "Why are we in such a hurry? I was very comfortable back on the steps . . ."

Aidan looked back to make sure Damon was following. Sure enough, the baby dragon was right on his heels, pitter-pattering now with a sense of urgency.

"Noam," said Aidan, trying to keep up with his nimble teacher. "I've never asked you about yourself. You have to admit, it's a little curious for a large mouse to be the keeper of the elf library."

The teacher flashed him a grin and just kept walking.

Aidan wrinkled his nose in frustration. "Please," he persisted. "Talk to me. You keep telling me to ask questions. Well, I have questions. For instance, why does the writing above the library say 'Hall of Judges'? That's a very important term from where I come from."

Keeping his eyes on the path, Noam responded. "Your questions will be answered this very day . . . if you survive. Heee heee! Yes, if you survive."

The Forgotten Castle

Aidan stopped suddenly. "What does that mean?"

Charles, who had been sleeping on his shoulder, fell off onto the ground.

"Oh!" shrieked the perturbed falcon. "How *rude*! You've got to give me some kind of notice before you make sudden stops like that!"

Noam also stopped. He flashed his yellowish grin at Aidan, who was helping Charles back on to his shoulder. He gave the two a chance to catch their breath. Then, he turned and kept on walking.

Aidan of Oren

Aidan tried very hard to get Noam to talk to him, but it was difficult to get a word in as Charles continued to complain about being dumped on the ground.

AN·ANCIANT·RUIN·LONG·FORGOTTEN····

The Forgotten Castle

They were traveling faster, it was apparent that the old mouse was now walking with a sense of purpose.

They traveled west through heavy woods until they came upon the ruins of a very old and very large castle, an ancient ruin long forgotten and not charted on any map. Large, intricately carved stones lay broken everywhere. A few walls were still standing, although badly cracked and weathered. Noam led them to a spot marked by an enormous stone arch, which sat at the base of a great mountain. The arch marked the entrance of a long, winding chasm. Sheer rocks shot straight up hundreds of feet high on either side. Noam took that opportunity to sit down on a large, flat stone and rest.

"Why are we here?" asked Aidan. He laughed nervously. "You were just teasing me back there, weren't you?"

"It is as I told you before. Yes, your questions will be answered very soon."

"What questions?" demanded Charles. "You've got to keep me informed about things, Aidan. I'm not just here to . . ."

They were interrupted by what sounded like the deepest and most powerful thunder Aidan had ever heard. As he looked to the sky, he thought it quite strange that there wasn't a cloud to be seen. Noam, still sitting comfortably on the rock, did not seem concerned. Aidan looked down and was startled to see Damon staring at him.

"Go!" said the baby dragon in a voice quite forceful.

"Now look here!" sneered Charles. "Babies do *not* tell grownups what to do!"

"Go!" said Damon, even louder.

"Damon," said Aidan, now quite concerned. "What's happening here?"

"Yes!" added Charles. "Just what the blazes is going on?"

Again the thunder rolled, shaking the ground and causing some of the large stones to roll around.

"Go!" Damon shouted. He pointed through the great stone arch. "Someone calls for you!"

"Oops!" blurted Charles, jumping quickly to the ground. "This is where I get off!"

Aidan looked back through the arch where Damon was pointing. He couldn't see anything, but he sensed a presence. He glanced over to Noam, who sat patiently on the stone. "I'm supposed to go in there?" he asked.

"That's what the baby dragon said . . ." said Noam with a hint of mischief in his voice. He flashed his yellowish grin in Aidan's direction. "I'd do as he says . . . yes, if I were you, anyway."

Charles stood on the ground behind the rock Noam was sitting on. He peeked his head out occasionally to see what was happening, and then quickly drew it back in. Damon did not move from his spot. The little dragon watched intently as Aidan gulped and approached the great arch. As he passed through, Aidan could feel the hair standing up on the back of his neck. The chasm was about fifty feet wide, but felt much narrower given the high, steep walls on both sides. Suddenly, the ground began trembling underneath his feet from a growl too deep to be heard by the human ear. The rumbling increased in intensity as Aidan rounded the first turn, then stopped as quickly as it had begun. Aidan paused. Then, a voice echoed from all around him … a very large, growling voice that sounded more like three voices than one. Aidan was so taken by the sound of the voice that he had not paid attention to what it said. He was filled with embarrassment, but there was no fear in him.

He cupped his hands and spoke loudly toward whatever might be around the turn. "I'm sorry, I didn't quite understand your words. Could you please repeat them?"

"Repeat myself?" came the rolling, growling voice. "Have you come here to insult me?"

"No! Please, let me explain." Aidan took one step forward. "Your voice startled me … it's like nothing I've ever heard before. It sounds more like three voices than one, and it resonates with an almost musical quality. Forgive my ignorance, I mean you no disrespect."

Silence.

"So, please, could you repeat yourself?"

"It was a warning."

Aidan again took a step forward. "A warning, for me? What kind of warning?"

"I warned you that if you took another step, you would be destroyed. And you have taken two."

CHAPTER 17

Magda

Aidan normally would have been sorely frightened by this, but for some reason his curiosity was peaked. "So you're going to destroy me twice, is that it?"

THUD! THUD! THUD! Something was coming around the turn. Aidan stood his ground, and for some reason still wasn't afraid at all. He thought about McKenzie. Wouldn't she be so proud of him? She once told him that she gave him courage, it sure seemed that way now. Then Aidan saw it . . . the largest creature he had ever seen or imagined! A dragon! It was as red as a ruby, bearing countless scales that shimmered in the daylight sun. The creature stood upright, its stature was surprisingly regal. The teeth . . . the teeth! They appeared to be as sharp as they were large. Not to be outdone were the eyes, recessed and black as midnight, and two large horns curved front to back on the top of the head, giving the creature a most ferocious appearance. The length of its tail alone spanned the width of the chasm. It was as magnificent as it was enormous.

Magda

It looked down upon Aidan and then again let out its deep, earth-shaking growl. "Destroy you twice?" it said, leaning down to get a closer look at the young intruder. "Do you know what it would be like to see the skin melt off of your bones? Do you know what it would be like to see yourself burning alive?"

"Well," said Aidan sheepishly. "Yes. Yes, I do know what that would be like."

The dragon sat back on its haunches and curled its tail around itself. "Are you brave? Or are you just foolish?"

"I am neither, I am simply Aidan. Aidan of Oren."

The great dragon snorted a puff of black smoke from its nostrils and lowered its head further, so that it came eye to eye with Aidan. "The child of Oren? Could it be? That would explain why you don't fear me."

"Actually," Aidan paused for a moment and bowed slightly, "I'm a little confused about that myself." He realized that he was in the presence of someone or something very important. "You know my name, but I don't know yours."

The dragon cocked its head to the side, obviously thinking. Aidan had seen Damon act in similar fashion when the little dragon was in deep thought. "I am Magda, leader of the guardian high council and mother of the great Algadon."

Aidan's heart raced. He had found the leader of the guardians! All he had to do now was tell the dragon about the war . . . the war back in his village, or time. Confusion overwhelmed him, and he could not find the right words to respond to the great dragon.

"I cannot help you, Aidan of Oren," said Magda. "I see your confusion, and I can feel the fire that burns within you to help your people. But you have passed into this land from the other side of time. The answer you seek will be found in your time, not this one."

Aidan was stunned. How could Magda possibly

know what he was thinking? How did the dragon know about the other side of time?

"Because I'm a dragon . . ." came the response to his unspoken words.

"You can read my mind?"

"No, I can feel your thoughts, young Aidan."

"What am I thinking now?"

"You're curious about the one I called the great Algadon." Magda smiled proudly. "He is the eldest of my six sons, and the greatest dragon that ever lived."

Aidan stood in awe, trying to picture the great Algadon in his mind.

"Yes, Aidan. He is magnificent. Much larger than myself, and he is very wise. In fact . . ." Magda reached her right claw toward Aidan. "What is that around your neck?" The dragon's hot breath steamed over Aidan as he stood very, very still. Magda gently lifted the necklace slightly from his chest. "No . . . noooo . . .!" The great Dragon bowed her head and let go of the necklace.

"What's wrong?" asked Aidan. "Have I offended you?"

The great dragon seemed overcome with grief. Her head remained bowed toward the ground. "There is much that you do not know, Aidan. It may well be too much for your young mind to comprehend. Go now, for I have no more to say to you."

"I can't believe you're telling me to go!" shouted Aidan at the now retreating Magda. "As you said, I've somehow crossed over from the other side of time. It's been a long journey, and I've put my friends in danger, just so that I could stand before you. And now, you ask me to go? I can't go!"

Magda did not respond. She walked back around the bend from where she had come. Aidan sensed that he had come too far to stop now. Although confused by Magda's strange behavior, he was determined not to let her simply walk away. He ran as fast as he could around the bend and soon caught up to her massive tail. Without regard for his own safety, he grabbed the tip of the tail and hung on with all of his might. He was drug over rocks and slammed into the sides of the chasm, but he would not let go. He was lifted in the air and shaken, but still he held on. Then Magda stopped. She lifted her tail up to her face and looked squarely at Aidan, who by now was badly bruised and bleeding.

"Why do you persist, Aidan of Oren? If you knew the truth, you would not pursue me. In fact, you would despise me."

Aidan opened his eyes, which had been shut tightly. "Let me be the judge of that," he said. "Please put me down."

Magda gently lowered Aidan to the ground.

"Why did you turn to leave back there?" asked Aidan. "What happened?"

The great leader of the guardian high council lowered her head. "Because, Aidan of Oren . . . because I saw my own destruction."

CHAPTER 18

The Story of Gog

ou saw what?" gasped Aidan.

"I saw my destruction . . . the end of my life, which I now know is coming soon. There is much you do not understand . . ."

"Then teach me!" Aidan glared up into the great dragons recessed eyes. "Teach me, please!"

"You are passionate, Aidan of Oren. Maybe you are worthy of legend as I have heard." Magda curled her tail around behind Aidan. "You need rest. Sit here on my tail while I tell you the story my mother told me . . . the story of Gog. A story as old as life itself."

Aidan sat down on the great dragon's tail, completely forgetting the painful cuts and bruises he had just been dealt earlier.

Magda breathed a heavy sigh and continued. "It is said that, long ago, stars fell from the heavens. In an age of strife and terrible war, dragons emerged. We worked with humans to create and enforce laws all around the land, which brought an age of peace and prosperity to all. Dragons were given the gift of strength and fire, so that no creature alive could defy us. We were also given the gift of sight beyond time, the ability to glimpse into the future. The picture of tomorrow was not always clear, but it was enough for us to choose wisely when it came to constructing law and policy. It is said that the dragons were a gift to mankind." Magda lowered her head. "I used to believe that myself . . ."

"I like that story," said Aidan. "But why don't you believe it any more?"

Magda exuded a low growl. Rather than sounding threatening, it contained a tone of utmost sorrow. "How could we be a gift to mankind when one of us has made a mistake that will forever doom the entire human race, not to mention ourselves?"

"What . . .?"

"They say those that possess great power possess even greater responsibility. Dragons had one other gift, Aidan . . . a forbidden gift. It was possible to give life where life was ending."

"Incredible!" exclaimed Aidan. "Why was it forbidden?"

"Because giving life meant giving of our spirit, and anyone who receives the spirit of a dragon also receives the power of a dragon . . . and much more."

Magda gently reached down and placed her hand under Aidan's chin, then pulled up to close his mouth, which had dropped completely open. Her eyes softened as she looked down at the young, brave lad.

"Wisdom comes by understanding, understanding comes by listening. Listen close, my young friend, so

AIDAN·SAT·DOWN·ON·the·GREAT·DRAGON'S·TAIL

you will understand. Dragons are different than humans. Humans are either good or evil, but Dragons are both." Aidan's face scowled in disbelief. Then he remembered Damon's face just the night before. It was ferocious, if only for a short time. He refocused his attention on Magda. "There is a constant war that rages within each dragon, the war between good and evil . . . it is the very thing that makes us fierce, yet good."

"What does this have to do with the mistake you mentioned? You said that a mistake was made, dooming the people . . ."

". . . dooming the people, *and* the dragons." Magda sighed deeply. "Seven years ago, a man lay dying not far from here. A dragon was with him, hoping upon hope that he would live, but knowing otherwise. The man had befriended the dragon many years earlier, and they had developed a very strong bond of friendship. When the man was close to death, the dragon mourned greatly, and swore by the heavens that the friendship would not end. It carried his dying body to the most heavily wooded area it could find to ensure secrecy, and laid him upon an old, fallen tree. Then, even though it was strictly forbidden, the dragon made a wish. Not just any wish, but the wish of a dragon. The dragon then consumed the man with living fire, and brought him back from death's doorway. Their reunion was joyous indeed, but they both knew that they could never talk about what had happened that day. So there, in the middle of the darkest forest . . . at the base of the dead tree, which now was curiously budding, they swore an oath of silence. It wasn't long before the man began to change. He took on characteristics of a dragon, and started growing in strength and stature. He developed beautiful white wings and scales, and found that he could do anything he wanted. Even though he was a good man, his new abilities corrupted him. As he filled his every heart's desire, he became drunk with power. His scales and wings started to turn black, and he changed in ways not familiar to a dragon. In fact, he grew to be much more powerful than any dragon who has ever lived. His pride made him jealous of the dragons, because they were the guardians of the land. He

wanted to rule the land himself, and he knew that dragons were the only ones that could have any chance at stopping him. So, one by one, he started destroying them. The guardians scattered, leaving their cities to fend for themselves. Most of the guardians have already been destroyed. Those that remain have gone into hiding, just as I have."

Aidan gasped. "You said that he was a *black* dragon!"

"Not *was*, my dear little friend . . . he *is* a black dragon. And soon, very soon, he will destroy me as well."

"No . . . don't say that."

Magda pointed to his Aidan's chest. "When I looked at your necklace, I recognized my own scale. I know now why you have that . . ."

Aidan was close to tears by this point. "But . . ."

"Do not shed one tear for me! For I was the one who healed the man seven years ago. I was the dragon that brought the curse upon all of us. So, you see, I have nothing to live for except to await my own destruction." The great, sorrowful dragon turned to leave.

"Wait!" shouted Aidan. "You do have something to live for."

Magda stopped. "What do you mean?"

Aidan ran to stand in front of her. "Look into my eyes. If you truly have sight beyond time, you will see that you have much to live for."

Magda lowered here head and looked deeply into Aidan's eyes. Her countenance softened, and great tears welled up in her recessed sockets. Gazing down at herself, she put her trembling front claw over her mid section and rubbed gently. "So, he *will* be born . . ."

"Yes, he will most certainly be born. He is my friend, Magda. I named him Damon."

The large tears were now freely flowing down the scaled face of the great dragon. "Damon. A strong name. You chose wisely."

"Do you want to meet him? He's right around the . . ."

"No, Aidan," she interrupted. "I cannot. We were not meant to meet, but what a precious gift you have given me. How can I ever repay you?"

"You owe me nothing, Magda, except your friend-ship."

Magda laughed through her tears. "You'll forgive me for looking a little deeper in your eyes than you may have wished. Yes, I saw my baby following you along through the forest, and I saw him destroy and eat a monstrous spider, saving a most annoying crea-ture . . ."

". . . that would be Charles."

"I also saw your fear, Aidan. The well in back of your Grandmama's house . . . you fear it even now."

Aidan fidgeted nervously, not knowing quite what to say.

"You fear that which you do not understand. Don't be afraid, Aidan. Keep your eyes pointed forward, fo-cus on the goal."

"That's why I'm here, Magda. To learn, and I've learned so much . . ."

"Oh, you haven't learned *that* much!" laughed Magda, now seemingly playful. "There is much more you need to know!"

CHAPTER 19

Secret of the Dragon Scale

idan could see that Magda was feeling much better. "You mentioned my Grandmama. You remind me of her in a strange way . . . and, you are right, there are some things I'm curious about."

"You are my guest, Aidan. Ask whatever you wish."

"How is it that a dragon can breathe fire? Birds have wings, and fish have scales, but nothing breathes fire."

"Good question, but the secret is really in the scale. If you hold it up to the light you will see . . ."

"I know," interrupted Aidan. "It divides the light seven times."

"Very good, my young friend. What you may not know is that it also magnifies the light, and the heat. Therefore, imagine each of the countless scales multiplying the heat of the sun seven times, upon seven, upon seven. Well, I must tell you that it gets pretty hot in here . . ."

"You're funny," laughed Aidan. "But, seriously . . ."

"I was serious."

"Oh." There was pause as Aidan tried to comprehend what she was saying. "You said earlier that you weren't surprised by the fact that I wasn't afraid of you. What did you mean by that?"

The great dragon gently patted Aidan on the head. "Don't you know where you come from?"

"Yes . . ." said Aidan with renewed confidence. "My father was a great wizard, who created my mother from the waters of Loch Myrror. I know that I am connected to nature in a special way, but not one that I yet understand."

"Do you know that names have meanings?"

"Um, yes. My friend Lilly's name means wisdom, and my friend McKenzie . . ."

"That's interesting," mused Magda. "In fact, I believe those qualities are also spoken of in the prophecy. But we're not talking about them right now, Aidan. What do you know about the meaning of *your* name?"

"Well, it means fire, I believe."

"Exactly," laughed the great dragon. "What significance do you suppose that has for you in particular?"

Aidan kicked into the dirt with his left toe. "Well, I have red hair . . . maybe it just means . . . um, I don't know."

"Think again, my dear boy. Although you indeed have red hair, there is something far more significant about your name. You are right . . . it means fire, and literally so."

Aidan paused thoughtfully. "Well, I have another question if you don't mind. I have a teacher. Well, he is a mouse . . . a very large mouse."

"You speak of Noam."

"Yes. Do you know about him?"

Magda sat up and gazed down thoughtfully at Aidan. "Mmmm, yes. Tell me, what do you think of him?"

"I think he's a little strange, to be honest with you," Aidan said with a chuckle. "I know that he's my teacher, but he's so odd . . ."

"Odd. That's one way to put it. But I prefer the term *genius*."

"Genius?" Aidan scoffed. "What makes you say that?"

"In your village, across the hands of time, does the Hall of Judges still stand?"

"Um . . . yes it does. But it's all boarded up. No one is allowed in there."

"Well, then, did you notice anything unusual about Noam's home?"

Aidan's eyes lit up. "Yes! It looks like a smaller version of the Hall of Judges where I come from! I thought that was a bit curious . . ."

"It's more than curious, Aidan. That building served as the very *first* Hall of Judges. All of the others across Lionsgate and in the surrounding countries were built from that precise design. It is now a library, a library that contains all of the laws ever written by the guardians. For now, they are useless. Noam was the one that brought the dragons and humans together. He is the one who put the guardians into place. Aidan, how old do you think Noam is?"

"Oh, I don't know . . . older than me to be sure."

"Well," snickered Magda with a twinkle in her eye. "It is said that he has always been."

"Always been? What could you possibly mean by that?"

"It means that, as legend has it anyway, Noam has been around since the beginning of time."

"That's ridiculous! No one lives forever."

"Oh, that's right, you've learned so much that you're *certain* of this. Am I right, young Aidan?"

"Well, I didn't mean . . ."

"It's alright. Noam is not the type to be offended by your doubt. I myself asked him about it once," reminisced Magda. "His reply to me was that he simply could not remember being born, therefore he had doubts that he ever was."

"That's funny . . ."

"Yes, Aidan, it is funny. Better to see it as funny than to doubt that which you do not understand."

"I like talking to you, Magda. May I ask you about something else?"

"By all means," the great dragon replied. "I am at your service."

"The elves have befriended us, and have even given us a place to stay in their village. However, we've learned that this beautiful land has a very dark side. Seven years ago, children started disappearing from the village. This horror has continued even to this day. We found out this morning that a little friend of ours, Frederick, has come up missing."

"Why are you telling me this, Aidan? There is nothing I can do. As soon as I come out of hiding, I will be destroyed. The black dragon is just too strong."

"Even you? You were his friend!"

"Especially me."

"Magda, the creature, which they only refer to as a Shadow, seems to be getting more aggressive. It came for me last night as my friends and I talked by candle light in our cottage . . . oh, it's afraid of light, by the way. It left deep scratches on our front door, I've never seen . . ."

At that point Magda interrupted him. "How do you know that this Shadow was coming for you, Aidan? Couldn't it have been coming for someone else?"

"Oh." Aidan was embarrassed by his presumption. "I guess it could have been coming for someone else. But who? And why? The only ones in the cottage were myself, my two friends Lilly and McKenzie, a falcon that talks too much and a white baby dragon."

"Aidan! Did you say a *white* dragon?"

"Yes, didn't I mention that? Couldn't you see that when you looked in my eyes?"

"Aidan, sight beyond time is not always clear, and it certainly is not in color. So, Damon is white? Oh, this is very bad. You both are in terrible danger. Go back to your cottage and make preparations to leave. You must cross the hands of time by the first light of day!"

"Magda, what's wrong? You're starting to scare me now . . ."

"Did you visit the Library, Aidan?"

Aidan nodded.

"Did you see the chest Noam is building?"

"Yes! I think it's the same chest that's in my Grand-mama's bedroom back home. I've never been allowed to touch it until . . ."

"Well, didn't you see the black and white dragons opposed to each other?"

"Yes."

"Aidan, that chest foretells of a great battle . . . a battle of good against evil . . . a battle between a black dragon and a white dragon."

"Damon has to fight the black dragon?"

"He is a white dragon, so I'm afraid so . . . but he's too young! If the black dragon finds Damon here he will surely destroy him. He will win the war before it even starts."

"War? What kind of war?"

"I don't know, Aidan. It could be a war of wills . . . a battle of intellect? Then again, it may be a battle of sheer force."

"Magda, tell me about this black dragon. Does he have a name?"

"He *had* a name," said the great red dragon as she shuddered with emotion. "As a human, he was known as Raven. He was a child of modest upbringing, much like yourself. Raven lived on the outskirts of Castle-dom, often traveling into the city just to behold its splendor. Although he was not of royalty, upon meet-ing people for the first time, he liked to refer to himself as *Lord* Raven because it made them take him more seriously."

"It sounds to me like Raven was a little insecure . . ."

"Maybe," Magda laughed a little. "That would explain his thirst for power once he realized that he had been given special abilities. Once he attained the qualities of a dragon, he left everyone, including me, and made his home in a desolate castle . . . a castle literally carved into the side of a mountain by an ancient civilization long since disappeared. It is a place called Dunjon."

"Dunjon?" gasped Aidan. "The Lord of Dunjon! He's the one that tried to stop us from coming here!"

"The Lord of Dunjon? Is that the name he has taken? I'm not surprised. Let me look again into your eyes." Magda lowered her head, again coming eye to eye with Aidan.

The young boy's heart tightened with fear as he remembered the obstacles the Lord of Dunjon had placed in their path only days earlier. The trolls, Kartha the deadly snake, the giant spider . . ."

The great dragon gasped and suddenly backed up. "He knows you're here! Take Damon and leave this valley immediately!"

"But what about the elves? They need help desperately!"

"You don't understand, Aidan. Raven is not only powerful; he is cunning and deceptive. He has the power to destroy you and Damon. Everything that you have fought for would be lost. You don't have a choice. As for the elves, they will have to fend for themselves."

"We can't just leave them!"

"You say that you and Damon are friends. Do you understand that Raven is *already* coming for him?"

"Then I will protect him!"

"Are you *really* willing to risk your life for him?"

Aidan's eyes lowered to the ground.

"Listen to me, protect yourselves. That's what I have done, and I'm still alive today."

"Yes, Magda, but what kind of life is it to be in hiding?" The great dragon was speechless. Aidan had obviously hit a deep nerve. She turned and started to walk away, when he asked one more question. "The children started disappearing seven years ago, Magda. Seven years! Could Raven have anything to do with this?"

The great dragon did not even turn to look back as she replied. "No, Aidan of Oren. Raven is not concerned with the weak. Now, go and do what you must do!"

CHAPTER 20

Noam Slams the Door

Aidan walked back the way he had come. His emotions were getting the best of him as he passed under the great arch, and said little as he motioned to Noam and Damon that the discussion was over. As they traveled back toward the Elf village, Aidan was torn by what he had learned. He knew that he must make a decision quickly. If they left, the elves would continue to suffer at the hand of the Shadow. If they stayed, they would all be in grave danger, especially Damon. Aidan's thoughts were interrupted as Noam poked him in the ribcage.

"Hey! What was that for?"

"I've been trying to talk to you, your thoughts are far from here . . . yes, very far away. We are almost back to the village. Is there anything . . . anything at all you want to talk about?"

"I wouldn't know where to start. You knew that I would meet Magda, didn't you"?

"But of course! Yes, it was time for you to learn the secrets . . . the secrets of yonder years."

"I've heard that somewhere before," said Aidan. "Why didn't you tell me that you were the one who brought the dragons and humans together?"

"Oh, hehe, you never asked. I would have told you if you had asked!"

"How would I have known to ask!" said Aidan, getting a little exasperated. "I can't . . . oh, never mind." They walked a little further in silence when Aidan remembered something he wanted to tell Noam. "I had a dream last night."

"Oh. Was it a good time?"

"What do you mean a good time? It was a dream."

"That's what I said," said Noam quite candidly. "Was it a good time or a bad time?"

"You have a strange way of putting things. It was a bad dream . . . a nightmare, really."

"Oh," said Noam. "A bad time."

"I guess you could put it that way."

Noam flashed over a grin. "It's the only way to put it."

Aidan smirked. He thought back to his conversation with Magda when they talked about Noam. *She called him a genius?* He laughed inside. They continued on down the path, and soon arrived back at the Hall of Judges. They decided to retire for the rest of the day and bid farewell to each other. As the mouse teacher slowly walked up the steps toward the large wooden door, Aidan called after him.

"So, Noam, should I still be asking questions?" His voice contained a hint of sarcasm. Charles, sitting on his shoulder, had to cover his beak with his wing to keep from laughing. But Damon, silent the entire way back, remained stoic.

Noam turned around and glared down the steps. "Do not make light of your situation, Aidan! There is a question that has haunted you since your arrival . . . a question that you're afraid to ask. The time within the time is at hand. I suggest you take this *very* seriously. Yes, very seriously indeed."

Embarrassed by his lack of respect, Aidan started to apologize, but it was too late. Noam had already entered the Hall of Judges and slammed the door.

CHAPTER 21

The Day of Stories

idan took Charles and Damon up the street into the Haven, where he could see that elves had gathered together for some kind of event. As he drew closer, he found Lilly and McKenzie sitting with the group.

"Aidan!" shouted McKenzie. "Hurry over here and sit with me!" The little seven-year-old scooted closer to Lilly, who was sitting on the other side of her, to make room for Aidan. Damon followed behind, seemingly curious as to the forthcoming event.

"What is all the fuss about?" asked Charles impatiently. "Why is everybody sitting here in the dirt? What are we waiting for?"

"Have we missed much?" asked Aidan. Lilly leaned across McKenzie and whispered. "You would not believe the wonderful stories we've heard. Most of the elders have already stood and shared a tale with the group. In fact, a few of the children have tried to tell stories as well, it's so cute!"

"She should have been here!" pouted McKenzie.

"What are you talking about?" asked Aidan. "I thought you were happy."

"I was happy to see you . . . but the Elf Princess is supposed to be here. She's supposed to listen to the stories and tell some of her own. They say she'll be here very soon."

Aidan's attention was diverted to the other side of the seated crowd. "There's Olivia! I wonder what she's doing here!"

"She's been here all day," said Lilly. She seems to have made many friends with the elves today. For some reason, they seem to like her."

"It's because she's beautiful," said McKenzie. "But I still don't trust her."

Aidan was taken back in thought to Noam's words. *There is a question that has haunted you since your arrival . . . a question that you're afraid to ask.*

"Hey!" said McKenzie, waving her hand in front of Aidan's face. "What are you thinking? Why . . . you're white as a sheet! Has something scared you?"

"Sorry," he said, catching his bearings. He grabbed McKenzie and pulled her across his chest and started tickling her. "I'm not afraid of anything, remember?"

"Stop it!" shrieked Charles. "Frolicking around can be extremely dangerous, you know. If you wouldn't mind calming down, I'd . . ."

"Easy does it," cautioned Lilly to the three of them. "We're expecting the Princess any moment now. We wouldn't want to make a bad impression, now would we?"

Aidan and McKenzie stopped playing, much to Charles' delight. Without saying a word, the regal falcon climbed down Aidan's arm and stood next to Damon where he felt much more safe. The children, along with all of the elves, watched and waited for a sign, even a small sign, of the Elf Princess' imminent appearance. But alas, Lira did not come. The air grew tense with anticipation.

"I've got a story," came a voice from the crowd. A murmur rippled through the elves as Olivia stood up and again spoke. "Yes, I'd like to tell a story if you don't mind." One elf started clapping slowly, then another, and another until all of the elves clapped together in approval.

"What is *she* doing?" exclaimed McKenzie in a loud whisper. "That is *not* her place!"

"Lira is not here," said Lilly. "I cannot see the harm in listening to her."

"Well I'm not going to listen!"

"Shhh!" hushed Aidan. "Don't be rude, this might be very interesting."

McKenzie shuffled where she sat, turning herself completely around in defiance. But the rest of the crowd quieted down as Olivia moved to the center of the group. Before she said a word, she paused and stared into the crowd seated before her. Her eyes moved from elf to elf, creating an air of mystery. Then she began:

'It was somewhat past night, aft long winter's day
So late that it seemed like the sun ran away
When the stars in the sky made a pact with the
moon

They would stay there forever, no more day, no
   more noon
The sun in his wisdom did not argue or cry
For he stood far away, far away in the sky
Instead he decided to turn out his light
To teach all the stars and the moon what was right
And sure enough just as the sun had so said
Without him the moon and the stars were as lead
Blacker than black, for their light came from one
One they had scorned, yes, one called the sun'

Not a sound could be heard as Olivia's story came to an end. The air stood still as the elves looked at each other with wide-eyed amazement. Aidan and Lilly also were spellbound, as was Damon and Charles. Even McKenzie, with her back toward Olivia, had tilted her head slightly to hear. It was a most beautiful story, and it was even spoken in elfin rhyme. The silence broke abruptly as all of the elves stood to their feet in wild cheer and applause. Olivia bowed in return for their affection.

"I don't like this," said McKenzie, shaking off the earlier moment of wonder. "Lira is the one who should have told that story!"

Aidan reached over and gave her a reassuring hug, although deep inside he had his own concerns. The remainder of the day consisted of more story telling by the elves, and Olivia, who continually surprised the throng with her unusual and mind pricking tales. Delicious food was brought out on exquisite silver trays, and at least for a time, the cares overshadowing all of them were replaced with fun and frolic.

CHAPTER 22

Never Forget!

Soon it was time for all to disperse. The day had come to an end, which meant that each of them needed to retreat to their homes and light their candles. Aidan, with Charles on his shoulder, Lilly and McKenzie started back toward their cottage. Damon was not far behind, and seemed to be in a very good mood. Suddenly, Aidan stopped and turned around, looking back toward the Haven.

"What are you looking for?" asked Lilly.

"You mean, *who* is he looking for," giggled McKenzie.

Aidan shot her a scowl. "I'm a little confused about Olivia. Just where does she stay at night?"

"That's a good question," said Lilly.

"No," added McKenzie. "That's a *very* good question. And, here's another . . . where is Lira? Why didn't she show up today? I hope nothing has happened to her."

Aidan said nothing more, but he was concerned. Something just wasn't right. They reached their cottage just as the sun was about to set. Lilly lit the candle, and the three of them sat down at the little table in the middle of the room. Aidan thought back to his discussion with Magda, the great dragon. Her words of warning were still ringing in his ears. Should he tell his friends about the conversation? Should he tell them that they must leave early in the morning? He battled back and forth within himself, not wanting to worry them, but at the same time wishing he could seek their advice.

"You look like you're carrying the weight of the world on your shoulders," said Lilly. Aidan smiled across the table, but said nothing. Lilly, sensing that he needed to talk, continued the conversation. "Are you worried about us?"

Both Lilly and McKenzie could see that Aidan was startled by the question. He cleared his throat and fidgeted in his seat.

Charles, still sitting on Aidan's shoulder, had no patience for the girls' concern. "Can't you see that he's just tired?" asked the falcon. "Aidan's had a big day, you know. It was a long walk to the castle ruins, my feet *still* hurt!"

"I carried you!" corrected Aidan, starting to perk up.

"Oh, *really*?" exclaimed the falcon. "What about all the starting and stopping? I even fell off of your shoulder once . . . I could have been bruised! And don't forget the fact that you left us outside the arch while you went inside the chasm to explore. Do you realize that we experienced horrible thunder the whole time you were gone? It shook the ground! Why, it was all I could do to avoid being crushed by the rocks toppling over all around me! Don't tell me I'm not tired!"

"What thunder?" asked McKenzie excitedly. "You visited an old castle? Can we go there?"

"Slow down," said Aidan, holding his hands up to prevent McKenzie's exuberance from running him over. "There's an explanation . . ."

Lilly reached over and touched Aidan's cheek. "What happened to you? Your face has bruises on it. I didn't notice it before. Your arms, too! Did you get into a fight?"

Aidan tried to think of a way to respond.

"It was the thunder," said Damon, staring up toward Aidan. "The thunder is the reason we came here . . ."

"This is getting exciting!" squealed McKenzie. "Tell us all about it, Aidan!"

Great anxiety welled within him. He debated over just how much he should tell his friends.

"It's ok," reassured Lilly. "You can tell us anything. We're your friends, and we're not afraid."

"That's right!" chimed in McKenzie. "We're not afraid of anything!"

Aidan took a deep breath. These were his best friends in the world. It was, after all, their choice to ac-company him on this journey, so they surely had a right to know the truth. He proceeded to tell them of the great dragon, Magda, much to the delight of McKenzie. He told them everything, including the part about the black dragon, and the danger they were in. Damon sat by the table, intently listening to every word. When Aidan was finished, the little dragon simply said one word. "Momma."

The room grew quiet.

"So you see," continued Aidan after a bit. "We have a difficult choice ahead of us. We could leave early in

the morning and avoid confrontation with the black dragon . . . or we could stay and try to help. I don't even know if we *can* help!"

"Well then!" cried Charles, who could stay silent no longer. "Obviously we need to leave this place! Why don't we go right now? I'll be happy to pack everyone's things and we could . . ."

"Aidan," interrupted Lilly. "If McKenzie and I were in danger, would you stay and help us?"

"Of course!" he laughed. "You're my friends, I would do anything for you . . ."

"Well, aren't the elves our friends?"

"Oh . . ." Aidan could see her point. "Yes, they are our friends, but you and McKenzie are my friends as well, I don't want to put you in danger."

"Friends stick together."

"Yes!" shouted McKenzie, holding her little fists in the air. "Friends fight together!"

"I said *stick* together," corrected Lilly.

McKenzie laughed and tried her best to wink at Lilly.

"What was that?" joked Aidan.

"I've been working on my winking. I'm getting pretty good at it, huh?"

"Uh, keep working on it . . ."

"I can't believe you're playing around like this!" screeched Charles. "I for one do not want to die in this forsaken land. Don't get me wrong, the elves are cute and all . . . but I think it best that we save ourselves!"

"I have to admit," said Aidan, taking on a more serious tone. "It is a difficult choice."

"Sometimes life doesn't give you a choice," said Lilly mysteriously.

"How do you do that?" asked Aidan, rubbing his arms. "You gave me the chills!"

Lilly did not respond.

Aidan yawned. "I think it's time we get some rest. Let's just sleep on it and make the decision in the morning. By the way, McKenzie, did you ever see Frederick today?"

McKenzie's face suddenly became sad. "Oh, I had forgotten . . ." She softly began to weep.

Aidan was stunned by his little friends' sudden change of demeanor. "What's wrong? Did I hurt your feelings? I heard about Frederick not showing up first thing this morning. I was hoping that he came later in the day."

"He's still missing," said Lilly soberly.

Aidan slid his chair over next to McKenzie's and put

his arm around her. "Don't be sad, we don't know that anything bad has happened to Frederick . . ."

"I know. But that's not why I'm sad." McKenzie wiped her eyes. "We learned first thing this morning that he was missing . . . I already knew that."

"Then why are you crying?"

McKenzie turned to face Aidan. Her eyes were bloodshot, and he could see that she was deeply troubled. "Because . . ." she paused and wiped her eyes again. "Because I forgot all about him!" She started weeping again, speaking between sobs. "With all that happened today, I forgot about him. We should *never* forget!"

CHAPTER 23

Stanley

hey talked for a while longer, consoling each other in the hope of a new day. However, no decision was made about staying or leaving. This, they agreed, was something they needed to sleep on. Just as each of them got into their bed, Aidan sat up and winked over at McKenzie. She smiled, and tried to wink back. Then, Lilly joined the fun, and the three of them spent the next few minutes unleashing a flurry of winks around the room.

"*I don't believe it . . .*" sighed Charles. "Our lives are in danger. Peril is at the door. So what do we do? We have a *winky party*! Oh, how my confidence crumbles . . ."

This made the children laugh. They talked a little while longer before the day was finally done. Aidan tossed and turned, finding it hard to sleep. On one occasion, he turned completely over, and was surprised to find Damon's head propped up on his bed. The little dragon was looking at him with big, sad eyes. "Momma," he said softly. He reached out and touched the dragon scale pendant that hung from Aidan's neck. "Momma."

"Yes," said Aidan softly. "I saw your mother today. I'm sorry you didn't get to meet her." Damon cooed softly. "She was magnificent. If you are to grow to be her size someday, we're going to have to find a bigger place to live." Aidan patted his little friend on the head. "I told her about you, Damon." The little dragon nodded as if he already knew. He seemed content, but a little sad. Soon his eyes closed and he fell into a peaceful sleep.

Aidan turned on his back, staring at the ceiling. What a day it had been. His mind was racing as he thought about Magda and the black dragon. Then his thoughts turned to Noam. The words of his teacher were ringing in his ears. *There is a question that has haunted you since your arrival . . . a question that you're afraid to ask.* He thought about Olivia, the mysterious stranger who said she had also found the little red door and passed through to the valley of the elves. He remembered McKenzie noting that Olivia's dress seemed to be too clean and neat for having traveled so far. He wondered why Olivia would show up only at certain times, only to disappear later. He also remembered the little cottage he found empty . . . the scribe's home. Something dreadful had happened. What was Olivia doing there, anyway? Noam was right, this was something that had haunted Aidan since they arrived. It was also something Aidan didn't want to think about. After all, Olivia was so beautiful, and her demeanor was so peaceful . . . she couldn't be bad. Or could she? *The time within the time is at hand. I suggest you take this very seriously. Yes, very seriously indeed!* Again Noam's words echoed within him. What could his teacher possibly have meant by this?

Aidan finally drifted into a deep, deep sleep. Even as he slept, his mind was trying to put all of the pieces of the day together. And then, Aidan had a dream. He found himself alone, outside, in the middle of the night. As he looked around, he could see the dim, flickering windows from the candle lit elf houses all around him. The sound of crackling twigs startled him.

"Who's there?" he asked as every muscle tensed in his body. "Hello? I know you're there . . . I heard you, but I can't see you." There was no answer, but he heard what sounded like someone walking away. He ran toward the sound, getting farther and farther away from the cottage. The sounds of footsteps continued. Even though Aidan ran faster and faster, he could not seem to catch even a glimpse of what he chased.

The pursuit led him to the cliffs of a high mountain. "Strange," he thought as his pace slowed, "I don't remember climbing a mountain." His trail narrowed, making the footing treacherous. Aidan placed his back against the side of the mountain as he worked his way around a rocky ledge. He moved as fast as he could until, to his horror, the trail ended. A few pebbles kicked out from under his shoe and fell out into the darkness below.

Stanley

"Oh!" he exclaimed, completely out of breath. "Where am I?"

There was no one to answer him. He realized that he was alone, and petrified by the fact that he stood precariously on a rocky ledge of a strange mountain. He couldn't move forward, and was too afraid to go back the way he came. A soft breeze blew against his face, calming him. He looked out into the strange valley with wonder. To the southwest, he noticed something glowing on the horizon. As he focused, he realized that the glow was in the shape of a circle. "The ring of fire!" he gasped. "It's real!" He looked the other way, toward the northeast, and beheld the majesty of Mt. Zorn and Mt. Zir, standing side by side. Looking closer, he noticed something unusual. Smoke was coming out of the top of Mt. Zir. Even in the moonlight, it was easy to see that the mountain was restless.

A small voice interrupted his thoughts. "Excuse me!"

Shocked, Aidan looked around, but saw no one.

"Hey! You with the funny shoes! You're in my way!"

Aidan looked downward and couldn't believe his eyes. A small rock, no bigger then his fist, had sprouted little arms and legs and was walking up the path toward him. It reminded him of Grock, the great sitting rock, only much smaller and with an attitude.

"What's your name?" asked Aidan, trying not to laugh at the hilarious figure before him.

"I don't have time for small talk, boy! Now, get out of my way!" The little rock had a squeaky voice, making him very funny to listen to.

"I'm sorry," said Aidan, covering a big grin on his face. "I'm afraid the path ends here."

"The impatient rock bent its whole body backward to look up at Aidan. "I know it ends there, that's where I'm going! Now, move before I make you move!"

Aidan carefully bent down and picked up the little rock. "Hey, not so fast, little fellow. Now, I asked you for your name . . ."

The little rock sighed. "My name is Stanley . . . and don't call me little fellow! A boy your age should show respect for his elders!"

"Oh, forgive me," said Aidan with a smirk. "Exactly how old are you?"

Stanley folded his little arms together in defiance. "I'm two million and something . . . I lost count. Now, put me down so I can fulfill my destiny!"

Aidan's eyes widened. "Destiny? What is your destiny?"

The little rock seemed greatly perturbed. "Why, to fly, of course! I've been waiting my whole life for this one moment, and you're going to ruin it if you don't put me down!"

Aidan looked around and up the steep cliff behind him. "Is this where the rocks take flight?"

"Not if you don't put me down!"

"Sorry," said Aidan, now a little more serious. "Well, if it's your destiny to take flight, I could just throw you over the edge . . ."

"Don't you *dare*! You'll ruin everything!"

"Ruin everything?" Aidan became very curious. He held the little rock closer to his face. "Please, explain."

Stanley sighed again and stood up on Aidan's open palm. "Ok, if I explain this to you, will you please put me down?"

Aidan marveled at the little creature. "Agreed," he said excitedly.

Stanley began to pace back and forth on Aidan's palm, and held a finger in the air as if teaching a lesson. "Of all the rocks in the world, there are precious few that have the opportunity to become more than they are. Let's face it, we're rocks . . . destined to simply lie around, sometimes, even roll around if governed by outside forces. But, to become more than just a rock . . . that's my dream. To fly like the birds, that's what I want! But, it won't work if you help me . . . I have to do it, here, where the trail ends."

"But, you'll fall!"

"No, I'll fly," said Stanley mysteriously. Those words! It almost sounded like McKenzie was saying them.

"Now, put me down!" insisted the little rock. "My time has come!"

"Alright," said Aidan as he placed Stanley down by his feet. "Be careful . . ."

He had barely spoken the words when the curious little rock with arms and legs walked away toward the ledge.

"Wait!" shouted Aidan, just as Stanley was crouching to jump.

"TO FLY LIKE THE BIRDS THAT'S WHAT I WANT!"

"Hey! Don't scare me like that!" said the angry little rock. "You almost made me slip and fall!"

"Sorry, but I have a question."

"Yessss?" coaxed Stanley.

"What does this have to do with me?"

Stanley broke into a huge grin. "Ha! You asked a question!"

"What?" said Aidan with surprise. The little rock sounded just like Noam!

"Tell me!" Aidan insisted. "What does this have to do with me?"

"It is often at the end of the trail that one becomes more than what they are . . ."

"The end of what trail?"

"You'll know when you get there!" The little rock turned to jump.

"I need answers! There are difficult choices I have to make!" Aidan demanded.

Stanley didn't even turn around. "Sometimes life doesn't give you a choice," he said. This time the little rock sounded like Lilly!

Stanley turned back toward Aidan one last time and winked.

Aidan rubbed his chin thoughtfully, and suddenly became surprisingly calm. "Hmmm, one more question, my little friend. How do you know that you'll actually fly?"

"Because *you* believe I can," said Stanley, now back in his own voice.

"You're right, I do believe . . ." said Aidan, still rubbing his chin. "I believe I'm dreaming!"

"Hey!" said the startled little rock, almost falling down backwards in surprise. "You're not supposed to know that!"

Aidan laughed. "C'mon Stanley, look at you! You're a rock with arms and legs! Anyway, I figured it out when you started talking like my friends. You don't even know them, how could you possibly mimic their voices?"

The little red rock leaned downward and kicked some dirt with his tiny right foot. "So, do I still get to fly?"

"Why wouldn't you?" Aidan laughed. "After all, it's your destiny, right?"

"But, you know it's a dream . . . that changes everything!"

Aidan nodded. "Yes, but what a fantastic dream."

Stanley turned back toward the ledge. "Well, I'm off!" He looked back at Aidan. "You still believe, right?" Aidan winked. "Ok, I'm gonna jump!" He looked back once more toward Aidan, who nodded and winked again. Then he jumped. The little red rock with his tiny outstretched arms and legs began to glide through the air as gracefully as a bird in flight. "Wheeeee!" he shouted, his little voice echoing through the valley below. He flew in broad, sweeping circles for what seemed like a long time when suddenly, he dropped from the sky. "Aaaaahhhhhh!!!" he screamed, all the way down. Bump! Thud! Bump, bump, bump!

Silence.

"Hey! I was supposed to fly!" came the echo from the valley below.

Aidan started laughing very hard. "I changed my mind, Stanley! After all, it is *my* dream, isn't it?"

"You're not funny!" echoed the irritated rock.

Aidan was still laughing as he shouted out over the ledge. "You should have seen yourself, Stanley! You dropped like a rock!"

The sound of rustling could be heard below. "Not funny, child . . . not funny!" could be heard in short, desperate gasps. Before long, and to his utter amazement, Stanley came climbing back up to the ledge. He was totally out of breath.

Aidan bent down and smiled mischievously. "So, my little friend, do you want to fly again?"

Little Stanley walked over and patted Aidan's foot. "I'd like to . . . but it's not my turn."

"What do you mean?" Aidan's face wrinkled with curiosity.

Stanley turned to walk away. "It's yours . . ."

Suddenly, the ledge under Aidan's feet gave way. "No!" he screamed as he turned to the rocky surface behind him, trying desperately to get hold of anything that might keep him from falling. But it was to no avail as Aidan plummeted into the darkness below.

"No!" He Screamed...

CHAPTER 24

Time Within a Time

idan's body lurched forward . . . his eyes opened wide with fright. He was startled to find that he was not resting in his bed. He wasn't even in the elf cottage with Lilly and McKenzie. Rather, Aidan found that he was standing in the Haven, just outside the stone house where Noam lived, in the middle of the night! His thoughts were racing. *How did I get here? How did . . .* The front of the stone building caught Aidan's attention. The writing above the door, The Hall of Judges, was no longer written in a strange language. He could read it clearly. *How odd. I could not read that this morning.*

CREEAAK!!!

The large, wooden front door was slowly opening! Aidan cautiously walked up the steps of the building and peered behind the door. It was very dark inside, the only thing he could see was the Dragon Chest sitting on a table in the middle of the room. Nothing seemed different than when he had visited before, except for now, there appeared to be a soft glow around the chest

. . . an inviting glow, which beckoned the young lad to come closer.

"Noam? Are you in here?" Aidan called as he slipped inside the door. There was no response. To his surprise, the room felt very cold. He wrapped his arms around himself and rubbed his shoulders as he moved to the center of the room beside the chest. Aidan looked around. "Noam? Hello anyone?" His eyes darted from corner to corner. A curious smile crossed his face as he realized he could see his breath steaming up in front of his face. "It's *cold*!" he laughed. "Why, it feels almost like winter in here."

Silence. Aidan kept looking around the room, waiting for his eyes to adjust to the darkness. But the far corners of the room would not be revealed.

"Noam? Noam, are you in here?"

There was no response. A chill ran down Aidan's spine as he was suddenly overcome with the distinct feeling that someone else was in the room.

"Hello? Hello! Is anybody there?"

Silence. Aidan glanced down at the Dragon Chest. The carvings of the eyes between the branches in the lid looked more real than he remembered. Then, one of the eyes moved and looked straight at him. Aidan jumped back, and then caught sight of something even more terrifying. In the back left corner of the building, he saw steam . . . the obvious breath of someone, or something!

"Hey! Who's there?" he mustered.

Aidan of Oren

Then he heard laughter. It was a woman's laughter . . . soft at first, but slowly getting louder. He looked down at the chest, which was starting to open slightly. A very bright light was inside, seemingly trying to escape. The laughter from the woman grew louder and unstable. Aidan was terrified to the point he could not move. But that voice . . . that voice!

"Aidan of Oren, behold your destiny!"

Aidan focused on the corner of the room. He could only see the outline of the person talking to him, but he could not make out the face. "I know you, don't I?"

"The chest calls to you!" came the voice from the darkness. "Within its chambers are the answers to all of your questions!"

Aidan's attention turned toward the chest. His eyes glazed over as he stepped toward the table and placed his hands on the lid.

"Yes! Lift the lid!" shouted the woman. "Lift the lid and you will see what is to be!"

Aidan's hands gripped the lid tighter. He wanted to lift it, but something was stopping him. A feeling.

"You're wasting time, boy!" the woman urged. "Open the lid now! Before it's too late! Or, are you afraid?"

Aidan refocused. He was not afraid to open the lid, and he would prove it. Just then, another voice stopped him suddenly.

"Not until the appointed time, Aidan." It was a man's voice. The tone was soft, yet stern.

"Where are you?"

"I am here. I have always been here." The voice seemed to be coming from all around him rather than from any direction.

"I have so many questions . . ."

"Then, ask them," came the soft reply.

"No!" shrieked the woman in the corner. "There is no time! Open the lid and you will learn more than you ever wanted to know!"

Aidan shook off the woman's remarks. Her words were beginning to slur into each other, and she was starting to sound crazed. He focused on the soft words coming from the strange man as he looked down at the slightly open Dragon Chest. "Not until the appointed time," the voice said again. "If you are indeed brave enough to ask a question, then I suggest you be brave enough to hear the answers."

Aidan's body tensed as he sensed the seriousness of the man's voice. He took a deep breath. "What has been happening to the elf children? I think Elijah . . ."

The woman in the corner laughed hysterically. Then, the man's voice interrupted her.

"Look with your heart, Aidan. It is the Shadow, and the Shadow alone."

"Where can I find this *Shadow*?"

His question was followed by silence. The woman in the corner stopped laughing. More silence, so he asked again. "Tell me, where can I find this *Shadow*?"

"I'll send him over to meet you . . ." said the crazed woman in the corner. A chill ran up his spine as he heard something sliding slowly toward him.

The man's voice rang out, this time very loud. "The Shadow seeks to destroy you, Aidan! You must leave quickly!"

"No! I have one more question!" The sliding sounds grew louder. Aidan could sense that he was in great danger. "Is my father still alive?"

The sliding sounds drew even closer, Aidan could see that the strange form, once in the corner, was now just about upon him. The form had many arms, but no shape. Aidan could feel it start to engulf him, making it difficult to breath. Suddenly, he sensed someone next to him, whispering in his ear.

"Yes, I am!"

Time Within a Time

Aidan sat straight up in bed, completely covered in sweat. His heart was racing as he wiped his brow clean. "Father!" he gasped. Looking around the candle lit cottage, he realized he was back with his friends. All was quiet. Aidan gathered his bearings. "A dream within a dream!" he marveled aloud to himself. "What did Noam call that? *A time within a time?*"

Aidan jumped to his feet and quietly got dressed. The night was not yet over, but he realized that the time had come to ask a very hard question . . . and he knew *exactly* where he had to go.

CHAPTER 25

Lor of the Door

Aidan quietly slipped out of bed and dressed himself. He was completely focused on the task at hand. The flickering candle created eerie Shadows that danced around the room, but they did not bother him now. He moved across the floor toward the front of the cottage, only to find Damon sleeping softly in front of the door. *He's too heavy to move*, thought Aidan, *and I don't dare wake him or he won't let me go.* He glanced over to the open window, and then down to the sleeping baby dragon. "I know you're only doing what you think is best," said Aidan softly. "But there's something I have to do right now, and I don't have time to explain it to you." He turned and slipped silently out the window.

He hurried back up the pathway toward the Haven. All was quiet as he half walked, half ran by the tiny elf houses along the way. He passed the Hall of Judges, looking back only long enough to notice that the writing above the door was still written in the strange elf language. As he made his way out of the elf village, he began to talk to himself.

Lor of the Door

"McKenzie and Lilly tried to tell me . . ." he said between breaths. "Something was wrong, and I couldn't see it. She was so beautiful . . ."

Aidan headed to the top of the ridge and passed by the little stone house where they had spent their first night. He laughed to himself as he remembered the dream about Camar, the winged horse. "Someday, I'll find you, too!" he said in jest.

His mind turned to the task at hand. "Now, where is it?" he said to himself. "I know this is the way we came . . ." Then, as he passed through a line of trees, he saw it. "There you are!" he said as he ran out into the clearing. He had found the old tree stump through which he and his friends had passed into the mysterious valley of the elves. He walked all around it and scratched his chin. "I think this is where we came in . . . but how can I be sure?" He saw no door, but that didn't surprise him, as there wasn't a door when they found it a few days ago, either. "Now, what did McKenzie say . . . knock with your heart . . ."

Aidan stepped back. "Sing? I can't sing!" He rubbed his chin as he pondered his dilemma. The night air was silent, except for the crickets singing in the distance. Realizing that he had no choice, Aidan groaned. "Oh, well, if a bug can sing . . . so can I!" He looked around to make sure that no one could hear him, and then, softly, he started singing. Badly.

"Ohhhh . . ."

Aidan quickly stopped. He thought he had heard someone groan. "Who said that?" He looked all around, but no one was there. So again, he reluctantly started again to sing, hoping for the door to appear.

"Noooooo ... please, I'll show you the door ... anything ... but please stop!"

Aidan stopped singing again, and the little red door appeared just as it had the first time. He looked all around. "Where are you?"

There was no answer. Aidan looked more closely at the tree stump. The bark was not like any bark he had ever seen. It didn't run up and down in lines, rather, it was twisted and turned. Aidan ran his hand over the bark, noting that it was smooth and pleasant to the touch. "What kind of tree are you?" he marveled aloud.

Suddenly, two slits in the bark opened wide forming large, bloodshot eyes.

"You're alive!" gasped Aidan.

"All things are alive," added the old tree stump.

"What is your name? I'll bet you are very wise!"

"I am Lor of the door, ask me again and I'll tell you some more ..."

"Oh! You speak in rhymes, just like the elves! How fascinating!"

The old tree raised its two shortened arms dramatically toward the sky. "Mystery falls as the morning draws ... I mean calls ... I mean ... oh fiddlesticks!" Lor scratched his head, or what seemed to be his head. "I mean, mystery falls as the morning falls, I mean ... ugh! And to think I've been practicing that!"

Aidan's eyes widened. "It's ok ... so you don't speak in rhymes?"

Lor of the Door

"Ha ha ha!" laughed Lor, startling Aidan. "I hear the little ones speak in rhymes all day long, every day! They make it sound so easy! I just thought I'd try my hand, or, uh, my limb at it! Ha ha!"

"You're funny," said Aidan. "I didn't know you could talk."

"Now you're the one that's funny! Ha ha!" Lor started waving his two short arms around. "I can't!"

Aidan scratched his head. "But, you're talking to me."

"Am I? Don't be so sure, my friend! Remember, you are special in ways that you are just now beginning to understand." Aidan thought about Grock, the great and wise sitting rock who had encouraged him only a few days earlier. Now Lor, the tree stump . . . what curious friends he was making. "You can hear me, Aidan, because you are part of nature itself. But no one else, not the elves, and certainly not your friends, can hear or feel the life force that flows through all of nature. It is a special gift for you, and you alone."

Aidan laughed and bowed playfully. "Well, then, it is my distinct pleasure to make your acquaintance, Lor of the Door!"

"Now you're getting it, lad! Ha ha! Now you're getting it! I was hoping that you might pay me a visit during your stay. Do you realize when you are?"

"Don't you mean, *where you are?*"

"No! You already know that you're in the Valley of the Elves. But look around you, didn't you notice anything strange."

Aidan looked up toward the twin mountain peaks. "Yes. I did notice that there are two mountains on the horizon. And I remember the words spoken by Sebastian Fry when he told us that this was 'an age when mountains touched the sky'. We seem to have traveled to an earlier time, when Mt. Zir still stood beside Mt. Zorn." Aidan stopped and took a couple of steps toward the mountain. "Hmmm, so Zir is *not* pushing smoke toward the sky. That's funny, I had a dream about that earlier this evening . . ."

"That's called a premonition," said Lor. "You'll find out what that is soon enough."

"Sometimes all of this makes my head spin . . ."

Lor of the Door

"Then let it spin, my dear boy! Better to try and understand than to simply stick your head in the sand!" Lor became more serious. "But, you didn't come up here to make merry with an old tree stump, did you?"

"No," said Aidan, glancing over his shoulder. The slight hints of light on the horizon foretold the coming dawn. He turned his attention back to Lor. "I have a question, and I must be quick about it so that I can get back to my friends. It is very helpful that you can talk!"

LOR, I NEED TO KNOW IF YOUR DOOR WAS LEFT OPEN THE OTHER NIGHT

"It is my pleasure to serve you." The old tree stump tried to bow, but loud crackling sounds stopped his progress. "Oh, my!" he said, rubbing his back. "Remind me not to try that again! Ha ha!"

"Lor, I need to know . . . did anyone else come through that door last night?"

"No," replied Lor. "No one else passed through the door."

"What? I knew it! I mean . . . Lilly and McKenzie were right to think something was wrong."

"What are you speaking of, Aidan?"

"Olivia! There was a strange woman who met us yesterday morning. She said she passed through the door to find me . . . but, obviously she was lying."

The wind picked that very moment to whistle eerily through the trees. Lor of the Door paused for a moment, then turned his big, bloodshot eyes toward Aidan. "It would appear that you have an imposter on your hands."

CHAPTER 26

Come for Me

The woman in the Library!" Aidan gasped as he remembered his dream.

Lor of the Door became confused. "What are you talking about? We didn't discuss any library . . ."

"Actually, she was more creature than woman." Although Aidan was speaking aloud, he was completely lost in thought as he walked in circles around Lor. "The Dragon Chest! She wanted me to open it, but someone told me to wait . . . my father!" He stopped walking. "Lor! Do you know anything about the Dragon Chest in the Library?"

"Umm, no . . ." the ancient tree stump said as he made a funny face. "If you haven't noticed, I don't get around much."

"I don't think this is the appropriate time to be funny."

Lor cleared his throat and tried to talk more serious. "My young friend, you must go back to the village and warn them about this! An imposter walks amongst you!"

Aidan of Oren

Aidan started to leave quickly, but stopped suddenly and turned around. "Who sent the imposter?"

The old tree stump pointed at Aidan. "You ask a question that you already know."

"The Lord of Dunjon!"

"Yes."

"So, he knows I'm here!"

Lor of the Door nodded.

Aidan looked confused. "I don't understand. Earlier today, I was alone with Olivia. If she was really an imposter sent by the Lord of Dunjon, why didn't she attack me then?"

"Maybe you're not the one he's after . . . the elves are a simple people, they could be easily swayed by a beautiful creature."

"No, I don't think he would bother with the elves," said Aidan, remembering the words of Magda, the great dragon. "He's come for Damon!"

Aidan turned and ran as fast as he could back to the Elf Village. Maybe it was time to leave after all. He couldn't let the Lord of Dunjon find them . . . why didn't he listen to Magda?

The sun was just about to rise as he reached his cottage. McKenzie was standing just outside the door, her eyes wide with fright.

"McKenzie, what's wrong?" he asked, trying to catch his breath. There was no response, although she reached her hands out for Aidan. He cocked his head, listening for anyone else, but heard only silence. "Where's Lilly?"

"It . . . it took her."

"What took her?" exclaimed Aidan, his heart starting to race.

McKenzie reached up and grabbed Aidan's face and pulled it only inches in front of hers. With her hands on his cheeks, she forced words through the fear that was engulfing her. "Aidan, do you remember . . . do you remember once when you said that you would always protect me?"

"Yes . . ." replied Aidan tenderly as he took a knee and put his hands over hers.

"What would you do if I was missing, like the elf children? Would you forget me?"

Tears formed in Aidan's eyes. "My little McKenzie . . . I would never forget you. If ever taken from me, I would move heaven and earth to find you."

"Then come for me."

"What do you mean?"

"Come for me!"

Aidan felt the ground underneath his feet begin to shift. He glanced down just in time to see something emerging from the earth. "A large root!" he gasped. Before he could utter another word, the massive root coiled itself around McKenzie. It picked her up and held her for a moment in front of him.

"Come for me . . ." whispered McKenzie one last time. As quickly as it had appeared, the root disappeared back into the ground, taking McKenzie with it.

"No!" screamed Aidan as he threw himself down. With his bare hands, he desperately started digging into the earth.

CHAPTER 27

Charles' Compassion

cKenzie!" yelled Aidan again as he continued to dig into the hard soil. Jagged rocks cut into his fingers, and his hands soon began to bleed, but he would not slow down. He was fraught with emotion, and in his frantic state did not know what else to do.

"Aidan."

From behind him . . . a voice, a familiar voice. He turned toward the cottage to see Charles walking out the door. "I've got to find McKenzie!" he screamed, starting to dig furiously again.

"Aidan, stop."

But he would not stop, he couldn't.

"Aidan, you won't find McKenzie or Lilly here. It took them . . . they're gone." The frantic thirteen-year old fell to the ground, emotionally and physically drained. Charles walked up next to him and affectionately tucked his head down and whispered in Aidan's ear. "You have to calm down, or we will all be destroyed."

As Aidan regained his bearings, he realized that the sky had turned dark. Heavy black clouds were overhead, and the wind was blowing furiously. Dangerous lightning was beginning to strike the ground near them. Aidan took a deep breath and tried to relax. As he did, the clouds subsided and the winds ceased.

"I don't know what it is with you and the weather," said Charles. "But one thing is for sure, we simply must keep you in a better mood."

The falcon's attempt to lighten the situation did not lift Aidan's heavy heart. He stood, dusted himself off and took a deep breath. "Thank you, old friend. Tell me what happened . . . what did you see?"

"It was the Shadow . . . it came just before sunrise. We heard sounds outside the cottage and we thought it was you. When we went to investigate, the beast was there. It was dreadful, Aidan! It came from underneath the ground and from all directions. Why, it was as if the earth itself had grown arms and attacked us. It took McKenzie first, and then Lilly."

"You mean, Lilly and *then* McKenzie."

"No . . . I'll admit that I was running away, but I'm sure of what I saw."

Confusion covered Aidan's face. "Where's Damon?"

"She . . . she took him."

"Who took him?" Aidan quickly shot a glance all around him. "Not Olivia!"

"No. Just before the Shadow arrived, Lira came and told Damon it wasn't safe for him here, so she took him."

Charles' Compassion

"Oh," sighed Aidan with relief. "We have to watch out for Olivia. I have very strong suspicions about her." He reached down and rubbed his hands through the marks on the ground left by their attacker. "I don't think the earth grew arms and attacked you . . ." he said as he put Charles up on his shoulder. "In fact, I'm beginning to think the Shadow is not a shadow at all! We need to find Noam."

Aidan, holding Charles securely on his shoulder, ran toward the elf village in search of his teacher. Surely Noam could help him find his friends. After all, Noam was the keeper of the law and the one who brought dragons and people together. He had to help . . . he had to!

As they arrived in the village, Aidan noticed immediately that all was quiet. He raced to the Hall of Judges and ran up the steps. The great wooden front door was already open, so he quickly slipped inside.

"Noam? Noam? Are you in here? I need to talk to you right away!"

There was only silence . . . followed by the sound of rattling chains.

Aidan searched behind the bookcase and found a staircase leading to a lower level.

"Do NOT go down there!" pleaded Charles, but to no avail. Aidan quickly shuffled down the steps, where they found themselves in a large room. There, in one of the corners, was Elijah. He was chained to the wall . . . the chains extending only far enough to allow him to look out one of the windows. However, Noam was not there. Aidan turned to go back up the stairs.

"FRE . . . D . . . K! FRED . . . R . . . IK!"

Startled, Aidan wheeled around. The creature named Elijah was reaching for one of the windows.

"FRE . . . D . . . K!"

"What do you think he wants?" asked Aidan.

"It sounds like he wants fried chicken!" protested Charles. "*Please* take me out of here!"

The creature stopped reaching for the window and took a few steps toward Aidan. He held out both shackled wrists and moaned.

"He wants us to let him go . . ." said Aidan.

"NO!" shrieked Charles. "I do believe we have enough to worry about as it is. We don't need the additional complications of baby sitting a four hundred pound shrew!"

"You're probably right." Aidan turned and bounded up the steps, but could hear the creature shaking his chains in the background. "We've got to find Noam!"

As they reached the top of the steps and headed for the door, Aidan stopped and looked back at the dragon chest sitting on the table in the middle of the room. "Seven years . . ." he mused. His attention was then drawn to the hole in the ceiling. The morning sun formed a beam of light shining directly down on the chest. Aidan had seen this before, but now it seemed to have more significance. "Seven years of light . . ." he said aloud.

Charles' Compassion

"Are we just going to stand here all day?" asked Charles, quickly growing impatient. "We have to find Lilly and McKenzie, you know!"

"Yes . . . we need to leave right away," agreed Aidan. As they ran back outside, they realized that Noam was not the only one missing. There wasn't an elf to be seen anywhere.

"Now, where are all the little buggers hiding?" sighed Charles. "I'm not in the mood for games . . ."

CHAPTER 28

The Puzzle

his is not a game," said Aidan as they explored the haven. "Unfortunately, this is not a dream either." They went from building to building, only to find them all empty. Pottery lay on the ground near the potter's building, and baskets were strewn around the basket shop. Deep scratches could be seen everywhere, the same kind of scratches Aidan had found outside their cottage door the night before.

"Oh, what an impossible puzzle!" moaned Charles. "We can't possibly find that which has vanished into thin air!"

"You're right, Charles . . . it *is* a puzzle," remarked Aidan as a light went on in his eyes. "So, let's put the pieces together and see what we come up with!"

They made their way back to the Hall of Judges where Aidan sat on the steps, placing Charles down beside him. "The children started disappearing seven years ago . . . which is odd because that's the same time the Black Dragon came into power. However, the Black Dragon would never concern himself with harmless little elves."

"Oh, Aidan, you're talking in circles! I can't help you with this if you're not going to make sense!"

"We've seen the 'Shadow', as the elves put it. But, it's not a shadow at all! What we saw were roots . . . albeit they were very large roots. Where do roots come from?"

"From a tree!" exclaimed Charles. "But tree's can't stick their roots out of the ground and take people! Even if they could, why would they? Trees are good, aren't they?"

Aidan rubbed his chin as he continued to put the pieces together. Then suddenly, he remembered the writing on the tattered scroll that Olivia had read to him.

'Age to age and fire to fire
Hearts arise and dreams inspire
When life and death become as one
The Shadow's reign has just begun
Until one soars where eagles fly
And brings the fire from the sky
Then the reign of darkness ends
Then the hearts of all shall mend'

"When life and death become as one," he said softly to himself. "The dead tree . . . the dead tree that budded!" He swept Charles off of the ground, again placing him on his shoulder, and hurried down the path leading to the giant trees of the Arboree. Charles protested the entire way, demanding to know more about the situation, but Aidan would not be slowed. As they approached from a distance, they could see a giant root sticking out of the ground, dangling someone just outside the tree line of the Arboree. Drawing closer, they could see that this *someone* was Noam.

"Be careful, Aidan!" cautioned Charles. "The roots look very strong indeed. If it gets a hold of you, it's not going to let go!"

Aidan ignored the warning and walked up to Noam, who was hovering about ten feet in the air. "Noam, are you alright?" he asked.

The curious mouse teacher peeked down toward Aidan and Charles and wiggled his mouth free so he could speak. "Oh . . . hello. It seems, yes, it seems this abomination has acquired a taste for rat!"

Aidan took a step back. "I thought you were a mouse . . .?"

Noam flashed his yellowish grin down at them. Aidan, determined to get to the bottom of the problem, rushed past the tree line into the Arboree.

"No!" screamed Charles. "Don't leave me out here!"

"Aghhh!" yelled Aidan just as he entered the dark woods. "Something is grabbing at my legs!" Just then, a giant root grabbed him and lifted him in the air and pulled him within the Arboree. A deep voice rolled out from inside the darkness.

"Do you like my garden?"

Struggle as he might, Aidan could not work himself free from the root which held him ever so tightly. As his eyes adjusted to the darkness, he looked below and was frightened by what he saw. Tree creatures, no taller than his knees, covered the ground. They appeared to

JUST THEN A GIANT ROOT GRABBED HIM

have misshapen arms, arms that continued to reach for him. He gasped as he also noticed that the creatures did not have mouths. However, they had big, very sad eyes, which watched his every move.

"Do you like my garden?"

Again, the voice. Again, Aidan did not respond. Rather, he tried desperately to work himself free.

Then the root holding him started shaking violently, twisting and holding him upside down.

"You cannot leave! Nobody leaves my garden!"

Aidan's pouch fell off of his shoulder to the ground. He looked down to see that the three peculiar blue stones that belonged to Frederick had fallen onto the ground beside the tree creatures. Most of the creatures were still reaching up toward Aidan, but he noticed that one particular tree creature lowered its arms and reached for the stones. It picked them up, then tried, unsuccessfully, to juggle them. It glanced up at Aidan with it's big, sad eyes, and tried again. This time, after dropping all three stones, Aidan instinctively started clapping. The tree creature immediately bowed.

"Frederick!" gasped Aidan as he scanned the floor of the forest. Tree creatures could be seen everywhere. He remembered his dream of running through the forest hearing children's voices, but not being able to see them. "The elf children! You're all here!" He glared into the darkness of the Arboree. "What have you done!"

"Do you like my garden?"

"Charles!" yelled Aidan, collecting his wits. "Come here now!"

"No!" came the shrill response from outside the tree line.

"Charles! I need you to come quickly! This is very important!"

"No!" came the response again.

Deep laughter filled the Arboree. Aidan tried to think of another way to call his pet falcon when he heard a rustling beneath him. He looked down to see Charles scurrying in past the tree people who seemed to be arching themselves, creating a clear path for the frightened bird. The falcon clawed his way up the root that was holding Aidan and crawled down far enough for his master to grab a hold of him. Aidan's hands were trembling as he held the falcon in front of his face.

"I'm glad you're here . . ."

"You look silly," smirked Charles.

"Listen," whispered Aidan. "I've never asked anything of you before, but I need you now . . ."

"You really should turn me over, I can't think upside down."

Aidan groaned and reluctantly turned the falcon over.

"Now you *really* look silly . . ."

"Charles!" said Aidan, greatly perturbed. "I need you to do something for me." He pulled the falcon close and whispered something into his ear."

"You know I can't fly!" screamed Charles in astonishment.

"Shhh! Listen!" Aidan tried to calm his feathered

friend down. "There is a time in all of our lives when we must become more than what we are. Now . . . this is your time, Charles. Listen, there's more." Again he whispered into Charles' ear.

"You want me to do what? Obviously too much blood has rushed to your head if you think I am going to go back there! He wants to eat me! Besides, he's chained to the wall!"

The root began to squeeze Aidan, causing him to grimace in pain. "Tell him Frederick needs him. I don't think the chains will be a problem . . . ugh!" The root squeezed even harder.

"You leave Aidan alone!" shrieked Charles as he jumped on the root and started pecking in vain. Laughter again rolled out of the Arboree. A new root emerged from the ground and swished by Charles' head, barely missing the falcon.

"Oh!" shrieked the falcon indignantly. "Now you're going to get it! I am a regal falcon from the royal family of Wingdom!" Charles stretched his wings out as wide as he could, winked at Aidan, and jumped off of the branch. The poor falcon fell straight to the ground with a thud.

"Charles, are you hurt?" called Aidan after him.

"Only my pride!" said the frightened bird, now scurrying out of the forest on foot.

The root holding Aidan drew him deeper into the Arboree. It was squeezing too hard to allow him to call after Charles. "Fly," Aidan whispered softly. "Fly!"

"Charles, I need you to do Something for me."

Aidan of Oren

He was carried into the center of the woods and placed down on the ground before a massive, misshapen tree. Aidan stood slowly to his feet, and a wry smile crossed his face as he heard something beautiful . . . the sound of flapping wings.

CHAPTER 29

Fill the Shadow

o you like my garden?"

Aidan dusted himself off, and with renewed confidence addressed the abomination before him. "I find it quite interesting that, although others call you 'the Shadow', you are not a shadow at all."

"Hmmm ... no ... but I like the name."

Aidan stepped forward, "Well, you can't have it!"

"You do not know to whom you speak. I am the master of this land. You will serve me, just like the others."

"Master of this land?" scoffed Aidan. "You hide by day, and strike terror into the elves by night! That's not a master, that's a monster!"

"You do not know me."

"Oh, but I do."

"That is impossible!"

"Is it?" asked Aidan, now jumping up on the root that once held him for a better view. "You are a tree that died long ago, only to have the living fire of a dragon bring you back to life. You changed, and became powerful ... and you became corrupt. You've taken elf children simply for your own pleasure. You are the author of a thousand broken hearts and an ocean of tears."

The giant tree was silent.

"Let them go. Let them all go now, and no harm will come to you."

"Let them go? They are here for my amusement . . . just as you will be."

Aidan heard the rustling of trees behind him. "I'll give you one more chance. Let them go, and live."

The giant tree started laughing. Slowly at first, then getting louder. Then it stopped suddenly.

"There is an intruder."

Loud slashing sounds and inaudible shrieks could be heard back in the woods.

Aidan was just starting to worry about Charles, when the falcon waddled through the trees and walked up to him.

"Is he here?" whispered Aidan.

Charles calmly hopped on his master's arm and crawled up to his shoulder. He started to say something when a large root wrapped around Aidan and lifted him in the air. Suddenly, Elijah jumped out from behind the tree and grabbed the root, snapping it in half as though it were a twig. Aidan and Charles tumbled to the ground.

"Yes," replied Charles as he ruffled his feathers. "He's here. And, oops . . . that was the last root!"

"What have you done? My roots! My beautiful roots!"

Fill the Shadow

Elijah, the warrior creature from the line of Cuchulainn, walked up and stood defiantly beside Aidan. He was wide eyed and breathing very heavy, with a hint of drool escaping from the left side of his toothy mouth.

"Did you bring it?" asked Aidan.

"FR-D-K!" mustered Elijah as he stepped back behind some brush. He reached down and picked up the Dragon Chest that he had taken from the Library and set in on the ground in front of Aidan.

"FR-D-K!"

Aidan pointed over to his left. "He's over there, Elijah. Just look for the blue stones . . ." The creature bounded through the woods in search of his elf friend, and Aidan turned his attention to the large tree.

"I will destroy you."

"Your days of destroying lives is over," said Aidan soberly.

"He's not so scary without his tentacles, is he?" whispered Charles.

Aidan knelt down beside the Dragon Chest and unlatched it.

"What is this? A trick?"

"It's not a trick," said Aidan. "It's fire from the sky. Seven years of fire, to be exact. I'll ask you again to let the elves go."

"Fire from the sky? You mock me."

"This chest contains seven years of sunlight . . . the one thing you fear most. When I open the lid, your days will be done. For it will fill the Shadow with the sun."

"Oh, Aidan, you're starting to rhyme again," whispered Charles. "You really should leave that to the little people."

"Fill the Shadow with the sun. No ..."

"I didn't get your name," said Aidan.

"Nor I yours ..."

"Then that is how it will stay." Aidan pulled back the lid, flooding the Arboree with blinding light. Charles tucked his head into Aidan's collar and held on as tightly as he could. All of the birds in all of the trees took flight at once, creating a loud, whirring sound ... and light found it's way into places it hadn't been in many, many years. When Aidan closed the chest, he was surprised to see daylight peeking through the trees above. The woods looked fairly ordinary, now, and all seemed calm. In front of him lay the majestic tree, now on its side.

"This is how it was in the beginning," said Aidan soberly. He reached his hand up and patted the silent tree. "It wasn't entirely your fault," he whispered. "It was a mistake ... a simple mistake. Sleep now, my friend. Sleep."

Fill the Shadow

CHAPTER 30

She Brings the Sunlight

idan," said Charles. "I hate to disturb you, but the tree people are still . . . well, tree people."

"I see that," said Aidan as he started visiting the tree creatures one by one. "Lilly and McKenzie are in here somewhere, but how do I tell them apart?"

"Maybe we should have twisted that nasty tree's limbs a wee bit more before we lit him up. I don't know how we're going to . . ."

Aidan stopped and stood straight up. "They say she brings healing."

"Who says . . . what?"

Aidan laughed and headed out of the forest. "The elves. They say that the Elf Princess brings healing. I remember McKenzie mentioning it. I'm sure that she can help us." They left the confines of the Arboree and immediately came across Noam. The ancient mouse was rolling on the ground, trying to remove the last few snagging branches still clinging to him.

"Oh . . . there you are," said the ancient teacher as he stood and dusted himself off. He raised his nose to the wind and sniffed. "Hmmm . . ." His whiskers started twitching wildly. "Don't forget to look under the sheet, if you dare."

"Hello . . ." Aidan turned around to see the Olivia approaching. She walked up to Aidan and Noam and stopped. "I thought maybe I could help."

"Where did she come from?" whispered Charles.

Olivia peeked behind Aidan. "It appears that you have found the elves . . . even the elf children long since disappeared. You are a hero, Aidan."

"Uh, hello, Olivia. Where have you been?"

"Oh, I've been around . . . watching." She took a step around Aidan to get a better look at the elves. "They need our help, Aidan. Just let me touch them . . ."

"No!" came a shout from up over the hill. It was Lira, the Elf Princess.

'A tiny touch, from this one fair
Will seal the fate of elves everywhere!'

Aidan took Olivia's arm and pulled her back.

"No, you don't understand . . ." she pleaded. "There is no time to explain, let me touch them!"

Aidan's grip held fast as Lira made her way down the hill and beside them. She walked up to Olivia and confronted her face to face.

'I'll ask you once, upon a star
Are you really who you say you are?'

"Well, no, but . . ."

"Enough!" Lira brushed by Olivia and walked over to one of the tree people.

'I will touch them, every tree

Aidan of Oren

Then all will be as it should be'

At that moment, something caught Aidan's eye. It was the sun. He put a hand up to block the light when he realized that it was not coming from the sky. Rather, it was reflecting from Olivia's eyes to his. He remembered McKenzie's words about the Elf Princess. *Some say she even brings the sunlight.* He thought back to the scribe's abandoned cottage, and remembered how the rain fell when Olivia started to cry.

"Look under the sheet, if you dare!" he whispered to himself.

Lira, about to touch the first of the tree people, turned around toward Aidan. "What did you say?"

"Um, wait just a moment," he said awkwardly. "Where's Damon?"

"Well . . ." said Lira, suddenly uncomfortable. "I'm sure he's out playing or something. Why do you ask?"

"I heard that you took him this morning . . . to protect him. You should know where he is."

"Let me touch the elves, then we will talk," said Lira, turning around to touch the closest tree person.

"Wait!" insisted Aidan.

"Oh," laughed Lira, "Are you having doubts about me, Aidan? Has the pretty girl with the golden hair deceived you to the point that you would sacrifice your friends? If you allow the imposter to touch these poor, cursed elves, they will be doomed to remain like that forever. Are you really old enough, or wise enough, to make that decision?"

Aidan did not know what to say.

She Brings the Sunlight

"That's it," she said softly, almost hypnotically.

A feeling of numbness rushed through his veins as Aidan's head started to spin. He needed a sign, something, to prove his doubt. Lira moved toward to the tree person that stood closest to her. Aidan watched helplessly, until he noticed that this particular tree creature was desperately trying to wink at him. "Elijah!" he screamed.

In a blink of an eye, the monstrous, toothy creature bounded from the forest and stood before Aidan, who was pointing directly at Lira. "Hold her, Elijah. Do not let her touch anything."

The creature pounced on Lira, binding her hands behind her back and sending her into a frenzy.

"You fool!" she screamed. "Do you know who I am?"

"No," said Aidan as he shook the cobwebs from his head. "But I know who you are *not*. You are *definitely* not the Elf Princess." He released his hold on Olivia. She nodded to him, then walked over to the first tree person and knelt down, laying her hands on its misshapen branches. Millions of tiny stars seemed to float into the air as the tree person changed. Aidan gasped. "McKenzie!" he shrieked as he ran over to hug her. Tears were running down his face as he held her tightly. "I'm so sorry . . . I'm so sorry I wasn't there!" Lilly was the next to be set free, and quickly joined her friends in a tearful reunion.

"It's alright," McKenzie said tenderly to both of her friends. "Everything worked out just fine, didn't it?"

Aidan of Oren

She Brings the Sunlight

Aidan of Oren

Olivia walked through the Arboree, touching the tree people one by one and transforming them back into their original selves. Sebastian Fry, one of the first elves to be cured, followed closely behind Olivia as she transformed elf after elf. He hugged each one, welcoming them back to form. Upon reaching the very last of the tree people, Sebastian Fry knelt down with Olivia. He tenderly held the branches of the first child ever taken . . . his own. He nodded to Olivia, who touched the tree and transformed it into Mathias, Sebastian Fry's long lost son. Tears of joy streamed down his face as he held his boy. It wasn't long until Sebastian's wife, Sonata Fry, joined them in tearful and joyous hugs.

Even Charles had to raise one of his claws and wipe a stubborn tear. "Oh, my," he said. "I wouldn't believe it if I hadn't seen it for myself."

"Believe it!" hissed Lira, still being held tightly by Elijah. Everyone hushed and stared at the imposter. Her mask of beauty and charm was now gone, revealing the evil and crazed creature underneath.

"Now, isn't that interesting," mused Charles. "Beauty is holding the beast . . . or is it the other way around?" Soft giggling rippled through the elves.

"Go ahead and laugh, bird . . ."

"I am *not* a just mere bird!"

The imposter glared at Charles. "Yes, laugh and make merry all you want! It's just too bad your little dragon friend won't be around to celebrate with you!"

"Damon!" exclaimed Aidan. "What have you done with him?"

She Brings the Sunlight

They were interrupted by the very loud sound of flapping wings.

An evil smile crossed Lira's face as she peered up toward the sky. "I think it's time for you to meet my master."

CHAPTER 31

The Black Dragon

The laughter stopped as a large, winged creature rose from the northern horizon. It looked like a dragon, only larger . . . and it was black.

"I don't like this at all . . ." whispered Charles.

Aidan reached up and stroked the neck of his falcon friend. "I was afraid of this."

McKenzie ran up to Aidan and hugged him tightly. "It's going to be alright, isn't it?" Lilly walked up behind them, and the three children watched in utter awe as the black creature drew closer in the air

"What is he holding in his rear claw?" said Aidan, squinting his eyes.

"Oh, I'm afraid it's . . . it's Damon," whispered Charles.

"Are you sure?"

"My sight is much better than yours. It's definitely Damon. He seems to be unconscious."

The black dragon descended upon a flat, grassy area next to the children, where he laid the slumping baby white dragon down on the ground beside a large rock. All of the elves retreated into the Arboree for safety ex-

IT'S TIME FOR YOU TO MEET MY MASTER

cept for Sebastian Fry, who stood defiantly beside Aidan.

"Leave him alone!" shouted Aidan as he took a few steps forward. He noticed that Sebastian Fry and Noam also stepped forward with him. Elijah, still holding Lira, moved closer as well.

"He will destroy you all!" screamed Lira. "He is the Lord of this land!"

"Silence!" said the great winged creature. "Your introductions are not needed!"

Lira quieted immediately. Her eyes were wild with rage as she fought to free herself of Elijah's grasp. It was to no avail, as the creature had no problem keeping her still. Olivia, the real Elf Princess, walked up beside Lilly and McKenzie and put her arms around both of them.

Aidan turned his attention back to the black dragon, now standing over the helpless Damon. He was about to run to his friend when Noam caught his arm.

"I have no advice for you now. No, no advice at all. If he were a regular dragon, yes, then I could try to talk sensibly to him. But he is not rational, Aidan. No, he is not even close to rational!"

"Listen to your teacher," insisted Charles, "and let's just walk away . . ."

Aidan shot a sarcastic look Charles' way. He reached over and patted his mouse teachers' hands as if to tell him everything would be all right. Then he turned and headed toward Damon.

"You are brave, but not very bright," said the black monstrosity as Aidan drew near.

Aidan ignored the comment and knelt down beside Damon. He could tell that his friend was still alive, which made him breathe a sigh of relief. Standing to his feet, he glared into the fiery eyes of the black dragon. "If you leave now, I will spare your life."

The black dragon tilted its head. "Your words mean nothing to me, nor does your courage. All that matters is that I have the white dragon."

The Black Dragon

"He's just a baby," said Aidan. "He can't hurt you."

"Ancient words are spoken of a battle . . . a battle between a white dragon and a black dragon."

"I see . . . and just how does the story end?" asked Aidan sarcastically. "Judging from your great fear, it must end poorly for you."

"I am not afraid!"

"Oh, but you are afraid! That's why you want to end things now. You have always been a bit insecure, haven't you, Raven?"

The black dragon took a step backward in disbelief. "How did you know my name?"

"I'm sorry, I didn't say *Lord* Raven!"

The creature growled deeply. "Can you imagine yourself burning alive?"

"Oh, *please* . . ." mocked Aidan. "That whole melt the skin off of your bones thing is getting old."

"Insolence!" screamed the black dragon. "Your friend will die now, as will the legend of the white dragon!"

"No!" Aidan screamed, standing in front of Damon. "You will not harm him this day!"

"You know," said Charles as he quickly jumped off of Aidan's shoulder. "There's something I have to ask McKenzie." Aidan watched as the frightened falcon ran over to where the girls were standing.

"What is it?" asked McKenzie as Charles approached. "What did you want to ask me?"

"Oh, yes . . . I was wondering if maybe I could stand *behind* you?"

The Black Dragon

Aidan's attention was drawn back to the black dragon. Smoke began to emanate from its great nostrils. It leaned forward for one last look at Aidan as it prepared to unleash its breath of fire. "You would die for this creature?"

"Yes," said Aidan in defiance, "and he would die for me!"

Just then, Elijah began to growl.

The black dragon turned toward Aidan's friends. "Hmmm . . . a descendent of Cuchulainn, no doubt."

"He is the last of his kind," said Noam as he stepped forward from the group.

"What is this? A large rat! I thought you were a myth."

Noam's hands were twitching uncontrollably. "He means you no harm. Nor do any of us . . . no, none of us mean you harm. Let us just go our separate ways."

"Do not take me for a fool, rodent! One day, the white dragon is to make war with me! Why would I listen to you? The other dragons listened to you, and look what has happened to them!"

The black dragon turned his attention back to Aidan, who continued to stand defiantly over the helpless Damon. "I have no patience for this. Step aside."

"I will not."

"Then burn!" The black dragon's words echoed down into the valley.

"No!" shrieked McKenzie and Lilly as the black dragon unleashed a burst of fire, completely engulfing Aidan, Damon, and a large rock that sat behind them.

Aidan of Oren

They could see only that the large rock behind them had turned bright red and was beginning to melt. Olivia, still holding Aidan's trembling friends, looked on in silence.

As the smoke from the scorched earth cleared, Aidan could be seen still standing over his friend.

"No . . . it couldn't be . . ." gasped the black dragon. "You are not natural."

"Oh yes he is!" shouted McKenzie. "Now you're in big trouble!"

CHAPTER 32

Destruction of Zir

lthough Aidan was still alive, unbeknownst to his friends, he was badly hurt. He stood upright and continued to stare defiantly at the black dragon, but inside he knew that he could not last much longer.

The creature, undaunted by Aidan's surprising ability to absorb pure fire, reached down and picked him up with his right talon. The claws around Aidan's chest dug into his skin, causing him to grimace in pain.

"Oh, so you *can* be hurt," said the black dragon as he examined Aidan from head to toe. "You are just flesh and bone . . . it was a nice trick just the same. I'm afraid your little friend will not be so lucky." The black dragon bent down and again prepared to release his fury on Damon. Elijah's growl became louder. Aidan looked over his way, making eye contact, and shook his head as if to tell Elijah to stay still.

"Although you aspire for much, you will never be one of the stars," said Aidan weakly.

"What did you say?" said the black dragon, taking his attention off of Damon.

"The stars in the heavens . . ." Aidan choked and coughed a little. "The stars that fell from the sky. They were a gift for all men."

"I am the most powerful of all dragons!" shouted the creature.

"Maybe you are, and maybe you are not." Aidan was getting weaker. "Either way, you will never be one of the stars."

"How dare you! I will *transcend* the stars!"

"Let me ask you one question then, if you're not afraid to answer . . ."

"I fear no question!"

Aidan coughed again. "Do you have sight beyond time?"

The black dragon became enraged at this question. "I am bigger than they are, and I am stronger then all of them put together! My fire is hotter than the rivers of Charon! I am better than them in every way! Why do I need to see through time when it is already clear that *I* am the future?"

"A real dragon can read thoughts and emotions. Can you tell what I'm thinking right now?"

The black dragon stared into Aidan's eyes, desperately looking for something. His anger was turning to frustration as he finally bowed his head as if defeated. "No, I cannot tell what you are thinking."

"Good," said Aidan weakly.

Like a bolt of lightning from the sky, the black dragon was slammed to the ground by a large red dragon. She stood over his massive, stunned body, pinning the black dragon's head to the ground with her giant rear talons.

Aidan tumbled to the ground beside Damon. "Magda," he whispered.

SHE STOOD OVER HIS MASSIVE, STUNED BODY

"Hello again, Aidan of Oren," she said. "You saw me coming, didn't you?"

"Yes . . ." Aidan let out a pained laugh. "It's a good thing *he couldn't!*"

The black dragon started to move, but Magda's hold on him stood fast.

"We don't have much time, Aidan. Although your bravery is commendable, you were not prepared on this day to meet the Black Dragon. He would have surely defeated you, which leads us to the most important lesson of your stay. Although a creature of nature blessed with special gifts, you can be defeated. You can die. Do not let pride blind you to your weaknesses. Rather, embrace them, as with your strengths, to understand your place in this world."

Aidan stood to his feet, not quite knowing what to say.

"When one day you journey back across the hands of time, go to the waters of Loch Myrror. Your mother awaits you there."

"My mother! She's alive!"

"Yes, Aidan, she is. She will prepare you for the road that lies ahead." Magda looked down with great affection at Damon, who still lay unconscious on the grass. Great tears welled up in her eyes as she turned her attention back to Aidan. "Every boy needs his mother."

Aidan smiled up at Magda. "Thank you," he said. "I can't . . ."

"Olivia!" called Magda, interrupting Aidan. "I need your help."

The real Elf Princess nodded, and instantly a great rumbling sound could be heard. Everyone's attention was drawn to the mountains. One of them was beginning to smoke.

"Zir is waking up!" exclaimed McKenzie.

"What are you doing?" asked Aidan, half afraid to know the answer.

Magda struggled a bit with the Black Dragon, now trying to free himself. "Aidan, there is no time to debate what destiny has in store for any of us."

"But . . ."

"Thank you for what you said to me in the chasm yesterday. You were right, what kind of life is it to be in hiding? Better to confront your destiny head on."

Magda secured her grip on the Lord of Dunjon. "I must go, I cannot hold him much longer."

Aidan was becoming distraught.

"Thank you for your concern, young Aidan. Maybe it would be good for you to know that I would have been here earlier . . ." the great dragon rubbed her stomach. "However, I had something very important to take care of first." She glanced lovingly back down to Damon, then spread her giant wings and took to flight with the Lord of Dunjon in tow.

"Where's she going?" asked Lilly, who was running up to Aidan.

"She's going to do what must be done," said McKenzie soberly.

The three of them watched as Magda flew to Mt. Zir, struggling all the way with the desperate Black Dragon.

Upon reaching its zenith, the great red dragon, still with a firm grip on her victim, dove into the open mountain, which had now become a live volcano. An explosion shook the earth beneath their feet, and they had to cover their eyes as they witnessed Mt. Zir being leveled to mere dust off in the distance.

"Ooohhh . . ." said McKenzie as she took Aidan's arm. "So *that's* how it happened."

CHAPTER 33

The Little Scribe

For a long time Aidan, his friends, and all of the elves stood on the crest of a hill near the Arboree and solemnly watched the smoke rising from the destruction of Zir. Many of them wiped a tear from their eye.

Olivia bent down and touched the sleeping Damon on the top of his head. The little dragon coughed, and then opened its eyes.

"Damon!" shouted Aidan as he helped him stand up. "I was so worried about you!"

The little dragon looked up at Olivia with his big, sad eyes. "Thank you," he said softly, slowly turning his head toward the smoke in the distance. He cooed quietly for a moment then bowed his head. "Momma . . ."

"She saved us," said Aidan. "She saved all of us."

Damon nodded. "Good momma . . . she's a good momma!"

He was patting Damon on the back when one particular little elf walked up and tapped him on the arm. "Well, hello," said Aidan as he knelt down. "What's your name?"

The elf didn't say a word. Rather, he reached inside his little vest and pulled out a torn piece of paper. He carefully reviewed its contents, and then slowly handed it to Aidan.

"I'm sorry, I can't read this," he said. "It's written in elf."

"I can," said Olivia as she approached. The little elf bowed as the Elf Princess came near. She gently lifted him back into an upright position. "That's not necessary, my little friend." Holding the parchment into the light, Olivia smiled as she recognized the writing.

"Well, what does it say?" asked Aidan.

"Yes," chimed in McKenzie as she wedged her way between them. "What does it say?"

Olivia laughed. "It says,

'All hail as the Princess is near
A stir in the breeze, tickles the ear
Behold her mystique, and skin that is fair
Behold golden eyes, and the yellowish hair
She comes in the night, not with pomp circum-
stance
With harm at the door, she can't take the chance
Soon, very soon, she will make all things right
On the day of the song, bid farewell to the night'

"It is good that the scribe kept this particular piece with him. Otherwise, I could not have moved about freely."

"But," McKenzie stammered. "You are a *good* princess . . . why did you lie about coming through the tree?"

The Little Scribe

Olivia put her hand on McKenzie's cheek. "I did not lie, precious one. Indeed I did pass through the door in the old tree stump, but it was many, many years ago. In fact, I was about your age at the time."

"It couldn't have been *that* many years ago," interrupted Aidan as he joined the conversation. "You don't look much older than us."

"You might be surprised," said Olivia with an air of mystery. She turned her attention back to McKenzie. "I'm sorry that I led you to believe that I had just come through the tree as you did. I could not reveal that I was from this time because the elves would have grown suspicious. As you can see, I don't look like them. Lira was a perfect imposter . . . she was exactly what the elves expected to see. Please forgive me."

McKenzie hugged her tightly. "No, I'm the one who was wrong. I'm sorry for getting jealous. You are such a wonderful princess . . . and your hair *really is* just like mine!"

"Who is this little elf?" asked Aidan as the little elf continued to stand close to him.

"He is the scribe whose cottage was destroyed," said Olivia. "He has the gift to write of things to come."

"Oh, the writing on the tiny scroll that you buried. I remember that you repeated those words over and over. You said you were planting a seed . . ."

"Aidan," laughed Lilly. "She *was* planting a seed . . . *in your heart.*"

"Boys!" snorted McKenzie. All three of the girls laughed while Aidan just looked helpless.

"Oh," exclaimed Aidan. "What about Lira, the imposter?"

They turned around and noticed that Elijah was standing behind them, empty handed. The ferocious creature was looking on the ground and seemed to be very confused.

"Where did she go?" shouted McKenzie. "Eeew! Look, by his feet! The ground is moving!"

"No," said Noam as he joined the group. "The ground is not moving. Those are maggots."

"Agh!" cried Lilly.

"Do not be alarmed," Noam continued. "She has simply gone back to her original form. Yes, the black dragon created her from larvae."

"I'm not surprised," said Charles, finally feeling brave enough to speak. "After all, she was starting to *bug* me!"

"Yuck!" exclaimed Aidan, spitting to the ground. "Sebastian Fry made me kiss her hand!" Everyone laughed.

The little scribe reached up and held Aidan's hand. "What do you want?" asked Aidan, surprised by gesture. Again the little scribe said nothing. He beamed a smile of approval, then turned and walked away. "What was his name?" asked Aidan, scratching his head.

"He has no name," said Olivia.

"Ugh!" moaned Charles. "*This* one has no name, *that* one was never born," he pointed to Noam. "*Dragons* were originally stars in the heavens ... am I the only one that finds all this a bit hard to believe?"

The Little Scribe

Aidan laughed as he picked up Charles and put him on his shoulder. "Hmmm, hard to believe . . . let's see," he mused, rubbing his chin. "I would have found it hard to believe that *you* would have been the one to console me when I lost McKenzie. And I would *never* have believed that you would ever fly if I hadn't heard it for myself!"

"Charles flew?" said Lilly and McKenzie together.

"Well, um, yes . . . of course I flew!" said the falcon as he puffed out his chest.

"I saw him," chuckled Noam. "It wasn't pretty. No, not pretty at all."

"Hey!" cried Charles. "Let's see you do it!"

Aidan reached up and stroked Charles' head. "Thank you, my friend. Today, you became more than

you are. That should be the hope of all of us, to become more than what we are . . ." Aidan stopped suddenly, remembering part of the poem written on the tattered scroll in the ground.

'Until one soars where eagles fly
And brings the fire from the sky
Then the reign of darkness ends
Then the hearts of all shall mend'

"Charles! The writing foretold that you would fly!"

"Oh, Aidan," sighed Charles as he rolled his eyes. "Don't get all dramatic on me now. After all, I'm not sure if I even like flying. It's really not my cup of tea . . ."

CHAPTER 34

The Day of Song

Sebastian," called Olivia. "I believe today is the Day of Song. Can you make the proper preparations?"

The leader of the elves turned and clapped his hands three times.

'From the forest, from the trees
All elves—let's fly like bumble bees
Hurry back into the town
Get fancy dress, and vest and gown
For on this day we celebrate
With joyful song and fun debate
We'll sing our songs into the night
Without fear, 'till the morning light'

A cheer rang out from all of the elves as they scurried back to the Haven.

"It looks like there's going to be a party!" squealed McKenzie. "Can we stay, Aidan? Please?"

"There's no hurry to leave," said Noam, flashing his trademark grin.

"But the war, we've got to get back and find the

guardians. I must travel to the waters of Loch Myrror to see my mother."

"No hurry at all," said Noam again, his whiskers twitching mischievously. "Those things you worry about won't happen, no won't happen . . . for about two hundred years. So, yes, you have time to enjoy the evening."

"See, Aidan? No hurry! I can't wait to hear all the music." McKenzie started dancing around in a circle. "They say the Day of Song is the best day of them all!"

"Hmmm, yes, that reminds me," said Aidan. "The first day of the Elf Princess' visit was marked with a feast. The second day was the Day of Stories, with the Elf Princess at the center . . ."

"I wouldn't have missed it for the world," smiled Olivia.

"Then, today, the Day of Song . . . everything actually worked out exactly as elf custom dictates."

"Of course," said McKenzie, trying to wink at Olivia. "I knew all along that everything was ok . . ."

"Oh, you did not!" laughed Lilly as she grabbed McKenzie from behind.

"Aidan," said Noam. "I am very proud . . . yes, very proud of you. Much has been learned in a very short time. You asked questions. Tell me, how did you know that Olivia was good, instead of bad?"

"You are a wonderful teacher," said Aidan as he turned to face Noam. "There were signs early on, like the rain falling when Olivia wept in the forest . . . when she spoke to the elves in story form. It wasn't how much the elves adored her that struck me. It was the way that she adored *them*. When I looked under the sheet, I saw was something beautiful, not something horrible."

"So you did not hesitate to stop the real imposter."

"No . . ."

"A good thing. For if you had, their doom would have been sealed forever."

Aidan's knees got a little weak.

"The elves are a simple people," continued Noam. "They embrace beauty and fear what is unsightly. The Black Dragon knew that a beautiful imposter would be the perfect messenger . . . yes, perfect indeed."

"That's why she didn't attend the day of stories. She went to get the Black Dragon . . ."

". . . who you now know as the Lord of Dunjon," added Noam.

"Well, at least we won't have to worry about him when we go back across the hands of time." Aidan stopped as he noticed his mouse teacher had started fidgeting. "Noam, why do you look troubled?"

"He has not been destroyed, Aidan. Slowed, yes . . . and you are safe for a time. But he will return, more powerful than before. Yes, more powerful and with a vengeance."

Aidan pointed to the now leveled mountain. "How could he have survived *that*?"

"He is more than just a dragon. Never . . . no, *never* forget that! He cannot be destroyed by force."

Aidan threw his hands in the air. "Then, what am I to do?"

"Magda has already told you what you must do," said Noam, turning to leave. "You must visit the waters of Loch Myrror."

"That's right!" he exclaimed. "What about my father, Noam? "Will I see him soon?"

"He's been with you the whole time, Aidan. He's whispered in your ear, and you have already seen him."

"What?"

"You will understand in time . . ."

"I don't want to understand in time! I want to know now!"

Noam paused and turned to face Aidan. "Is it not enough to know that he has been with you, helping you every step of the way?"

Aidan paced anxiously in a circle. "No, it's not enough! Tell me, where is he?"

"He just left."

"What?" Aidan looked in all directions. "The scribe!" He ran in the direction the little elf had departed, but could find no one. Then he remembered the cottage with the overturned table. Traveling as quickly as he could, he found the place on the path where he had entered the woods only the day before. He rushed in, beating back the heavy brush that seemed intent on slowing him down.

"Where are you?" he called aloud, still desperately searching for the cottage. He continued deeper and deeper into the woods, but the cottage was not there, and Aidan soon found that he was hopelessly lost. Suddenly, he heard music. It was beautiful, and it was coming from all around him.

"The Day of Song!" he exclaimed. He tried to walk in the direction of the sound, but ended up walking in a large circle. His breath was heavy with exasperation, and he was on the verge of panic when he heard a voice.

"Aidan of Oren, what is it that you seek?"

He spun around to see Olivia standing behind him.

"I'm looking for my father. Please, can you help me?"

"You have already found him. And, he has found you."

"I know . . ." said Aidan, still frustrated. "But I want to talk to him. I have so much I want to ask him."

"For everything there is a season." Her words were soothing and calming to Aidan. He started to breathe easier. "You have found the elves, in more ways than one. You have learned the secrets of old, and you now know why the guardians disappeared. It is enough."

"But what are we to do tomorrow?"

"Do not fret for tomorrow, Aidan. Tomorrow will take care of itself."

"When should we go back?"

"You'll know when the time is right." She looked tenderly into his eyes. "Your mother will be waiting for you, as will your father."

"But, my father is here!"

"Not anymore."

The Day of Song

Aidan shook his head. "A scribe. My father is an elf scribe?"

Olivia laughed. "Your father is many things. Soon you will understand." The Elf Princess stared thoughtfully into Aidan's eyes. "Come, take my hand. I want to show you something."

Aidan reached over and took Olivia's fair hand in his.

"Now, close your eyes."

As Aidan closed his eyes, a whirlwind of images filled his senses. He saw McKenzie laughing and dancing with Frederick, Sebastian Fry and his family. Lilly was singing most beautifully with an ensemble of elf musicians, while Damon and Charles were frolicking with the elf children. Then, as if looking down from the sky, he beheld the valley of the elves. The sun was just beginning to rise, flooding the valley with radiant light. He could hear the Elf Princess whisper:

'The rise of the sun is the rise of a man
A man who now holds the stars in his hand'

Aidan opened his eyes. They had not moved, although he was sure they had. "What just happened?" he asked.

"The dancing, the singing, and the light that now floods the valley are all because of you, Aidan." She started walking to her left, gently pulling Aidan by the hand. "It is the Day of Song, the others are waiting. Let us rejoice with the elves and sing the songs of old."

Aidan offered no resistance. Together, he and the Elf Princess walked back to the village, and back to the elves that would declare his praise. Back to Noam, who would be anxious to continue the lessons in the library, and back to his friends, which were now much more than friends . . . they were his family.

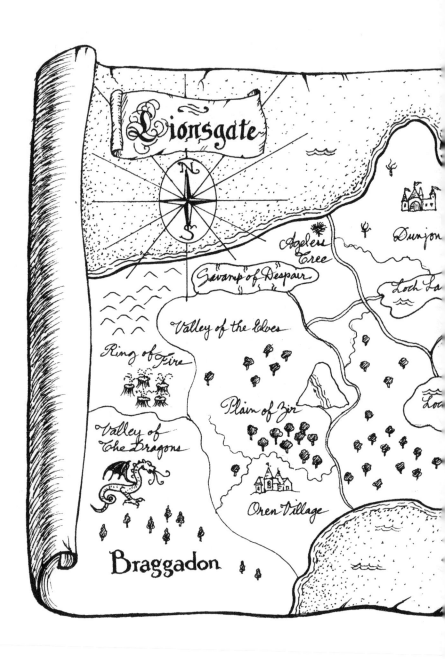

Goth

Morrow Sea

Olsburg

Stonebridge

Casteldom

Abyss of Charon

Rock of Algamon

...ted Caverns

Plain of Capricorn

Gilan Desert

Land's End

Bothan Sea